LIFE ON EARTH

CONTENTS

WHERE DID DINOSAURS GO?

Mike Unwin

Designed by Ian McNee

**Illustrated by Andrew Robinson,
Toni Goffe and Guy Smith**

Edited by Cheryl Evans

**Consultant: Dr Angela Milner
(The Natural History Museum, London)**

CONTENTS

What were dinosaurs?

Dinosaurs were animals that lived millions of years ago, before there were any people. Today there are no dinosaurs left.

Stegosaurus was a dinosaur that lived 150 million years ago.

Dinosaur means 'terrible lizard'. People called them this because their skeletons looked like giant lizards' skeletons.

Now scientists know that dinosaurs were not lizards. This part of the book explains what they really were.

Giants

Most dinosaurs were much bigger than the lizards you can see today.

Diplodocus was one of the longest dinosaurs. It grew up to 27m (89ft) long. That's as long as a tennis court.

The Komodo Dragon is the longest lizard alive today. It grows up to 3m (10ft) long.

65 million years ago dinosaurs became extinct. This means they disappeared forever. Nobody is sure why this happened. But experts have many ideas about it, as you will discover in this part of the book.

A long time ago

The time before people began to write is called prehistory. It is split into three different parts called eras. This picture tells you a little about each one.

225 million years ago.

Paleozoic Era

Trilobites were small creatures that lived in the sea during the Paleozoic Era. This was before dinosaurs.

Dinosaurs appeared here.

This arrow has colors to show the different eras.

Dinosaurs disappeared here.

Mesozoic Era

Dinosaurs lived during the Mesozoic Era. This era can be split up into three different periods. Here you can see a dinosaur from each period.

Plateosaurus lived during the Triassic Period.

Dinosaurs were prehistoric animals that lived on Earth for 154 million years. People have only been around for about the last three million years.

Allosaurus lived during the Jurassic Period.

Cenozoic Era

Brontotherium was a big animal that lived during the Cenozoic Era. This was after dinosaurs.

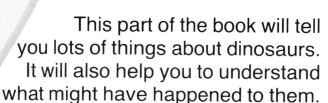

Styracosaurus lived during the Cretaceous Period.

65 million years ago.

People appeared about three million years ago.

People have not been here for long compared to dinosaurs.

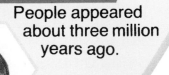

This part of the book will tell you lots of things about dinosaurs. It will also help you to understand what might have happened to them.

3

What's left of dinosaurs

Experts have learned about dinosaurs by studying fossils. Fossils are the remains of animals that died a long time ago and have been turned into stone. They are all that is left of the dinosaurs now.

How fossils were made

When a dinosaur died, its soft parts soon rotted away. But its hard skeleton was left.

If the dinosaur was in a muddy place such as the bottom of a lake, the skeleton sank into the mud.

As more mud covered the skeleton, the bottom layers were squashed and hardened into rock.

Over time, special minerals in the rock turned the skeleton to stone. This made it into a fossil.

Dinosaur jigsaw puzzle

Scientists who study fossils are called paleontologists. They try to fit all the fossil pieces of a dinosaur together to find out what it looked like and figure out how it lived.

This rock is 150 million years old.

A special hammer is used to chip rock from around the bones.

Paleontologists photograph each fossil before they remove it, so they know exactly where it was found.

Fossils are found in places that were once covered by water. Here you can see a dinosaur fossil being dug out of a cliff.

Getting it wrong

Sometimes paleontologists make mistakes. When scientists first put *Iguanodon* together, they found one bone that did not seem to fit the rest of the skeleton. They decided that it belonged on *Iguanodon*'s nose, like a rhinoceros's horn. But when they found more fossils they realized that this bone was a spike on *Iguanodon*'s thumb.

At first they thought *Iguanodon* looked something like this.

This is the bone that confused scientists.

Now they know *Iguanodon* looked more like this.

Experts wrap fossils in damp paper and plaster to protect them. Each one is given a number.

Fossils are packed and then taken away to be studied.

More to come

In 1965, paleontologists in Mongolia found the huge arms of a dinosaur they called *Deinocheirus*. They are still looking for its body.

Deinocheirus's arms were longer than a man.

5

Dinosaur origins

It helps to understand why dinosaurs disappeared if you know where they came from. Most scientists think all living things gradually change. This change is called evolution.

Your environment is the area where you live. Evolution makes animals change, or evolve, to suit their environment.

Giraffes live in an environment with tall trees. They have evolved long necks to reach the leaves at the top.

From water to land

Here you can see how dinosaurs evolved over millions of years.

Over 350 million years ago, no animals lived on the land. But where pools began to dry up, some fish began to leave the water.

Eusthenopteron was a fish that used its strong fins like legs.

How to survive

Sometimes environments can change. Animals that are suited to the changes survive, but others die. A famous scientist, Charles Darwin, called this natural selection.

Not everybody believes in evolution and natural selection. Many people believe God created Earth and put animals on it as they are now.

350 million years ago, animals with legs, called amphibians, evolved. They lived on land, but they had to be close to water to lay eggs.

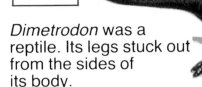

Dimetrodon was a reptile. Its legs stuck out from the sides of its body.

Ichthyostega was an amphibian. Its legs carried it low over the ground.

310 million years ago, animals called reptiles evolved. Their bodies were now suited to life on the land. They had dry, scaly skin to protect them from the sun.

230 million years ago, some reptiles evolved stronger and straighter legs. These were the first dinosaurs.

Natural selection at work

Peppered Moths show how a changing environment can make animals evolve.

3. When factories were built, smoke made the trees darker. Birds now found it easier to catch pale moths.

1. Some Peppered Moths are dark and some are pale. 200 years ago there were more pale moths.

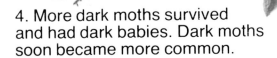

2. Pale moths were the same color as trees, so birds caught more dark ones, which were easier to see.

4. More dark moths survived and had dark babies. Dark moths soon became more common.

7

Shapes and sizes

Dinosaurs evolved into many different sizes. Some were quite small. Others were much bigger than any land animals alive today.

Brachiosaurus was one of the biggest dinosaurs. It could weigh more than 50 tonnes (51 tons). That's the same as nine elephants.

Brachiosaurus was as high as a three story house.

Its back bones were light but very strong to help carry its heavy body.

Strong legs supported its weight.

Keeping warm

Animals cannot survive if they get too hot or too cold. A dinosaur's temperature changed with the heat of the Sun. In cool weather, dinosaurs got cold.

The biggest dinosaurs were so huge that it took them a very long time to cool down. So their great size helped them to keep warm.

Using a sail

Spinosaurus had a special sail on its back to keep its body at the right temperature. As the Sun moved, *Spinosaurus* changed position.

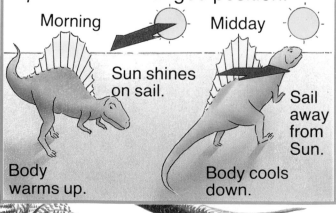

Morning

Sun shines on sail.

Midday

Sail away from Sun.

Body warms up.

Body cools down.

Different shapes

Dinosaurs evolved into different shapes for different reasons.

Ceratopians had huge heads with bony frills and sharp horns. *Triceratops* was the biggest ceratopian. It was 11m (36ft) long and weighed 5.4 tonnes (6 tons).

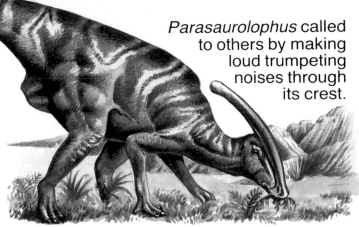

Parasaurolophus called to others by making loud trumpeting noises through its crest.

Parasaurolophus had a bony beak for tearing off plants to eat, and a bony crest on its head.

Triceratops had sharp horns to keep enemies away.

A bony frill protected its neck and held strong muscles for working its jaws.

Euplocephalus was a heavy dinosaur covered in armor and spikes for protection.

Euplocephalus used its tail as a club to defend itself.

Make a dinosaur

You could make a *Euplocephalus* with balls of playdough, used matches and drawing pins.

Roll a big ball for the body.

Roll smaller balls for the head, legs and club.

Roll a sausage shape for the tail.

Use broken matches for the spikes.

Use drawing pins for the armour.

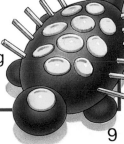

9

Dinosaur life

Fossil clues help experts to find out how dinosaurs lived. This also helps them to discover what changes may have made dinosaurs die out.

Clues about food

Some dinosaurs had sharp teeth and strong claws. This shows that they ate meat. *Tyrannosaurus rex* was one of the biggest meat-eaters ever. It was as heavy as an elephant and as long as a bus.

Tyrannosaurus rex had sharp teeth for cutting meat.

How you eat

People can eat many different kinds of food. You have different teeth for different jobs. Look at your mouth in a mirror and feel inside with clean fingers.

Can you feel sharp front teeth for cutting and knobbly back teeth for grinding?

Other dinosaurs had special teeth for eating plants. *Corythosaurus* was a plant-eater. It chewed on tough leaves and twigs.

Corythosaurus's jawbone shows hundreds of small teeth for grinding plants.

Strong claws for tearing open its prey.

Corythosaurus

Fossil dinosaur droppings can show what dinosaurs ate.

Pine needles in dropping.

Eggs

Scientists know that some dinosaurs laid eggs, because they have found lots of fossil ones. The biggest eggs are over 30cm (1ft) across.

Baby *Protoceratops* hatched from eggs laid in the sand to keep them warm.

Staying together

Lots of fossil *Triceratops* have been found together. This shows that they probably lived in herds.

Experts think adult *Triceratops* surrounded their babies to protect them from danger.

Fossil footprints

Velociraptor was a fierce hunter. It was only two meters (6.5ft) long, but its fossil footprints are spaced far apart. This shows how fast *Velociraptor* could run.

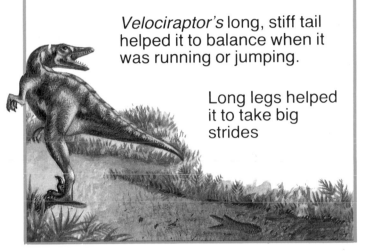

Velociraptor's long, stiff tail helped it to balance when it was running or jumping.

Long legs helped it to take big strides

Fighting

Some dinosaurs that lived in herds fought each other to decide upon a leader. The thick skull bone of the male *Pachycephalosaurus* was probably used to protect it in fights.

Pachycephalosaurus fought with their heads, like goats do.

11

Alongside dinosaurs

While dinosaurs were living on the land, other prehistoric reptiles were living in the sea and the air. Interestingly, they disappeared at exactly the same time as dinosaurs.

Sea monsters

Huge reptiles lived in the sea. Their long, smooth bodies made them good swimmers. Their legs evolved into flippers to help them swim.

Ichthyosaurs grew up to 12m (38ft) long. They did not lay eggs, but gave birth to their young underwater.

Large flippers pulled plesiosaurs through the water.

Long necks helped them to catch fish.

Plesiosaurs grew up to 12m (38ft) long. They came onto land to lay their eggs.

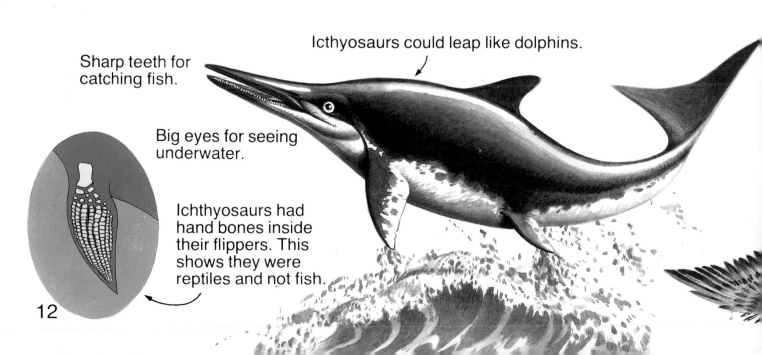

Icthyosaurs could leap like dolphins.

Sharp teeth for catching fish.

Big eyes for seeing underwater.

Ichthyosaurs had hand bones inside their flippers. This shows they were reptiles and not fish.

In the air

Pterosaurs were flying reptiles. They had wings made of skin, just like bats today. They also had very light bones to help them fly. Some were no bigger than a sparrow. Others were the size of a small aircraft.

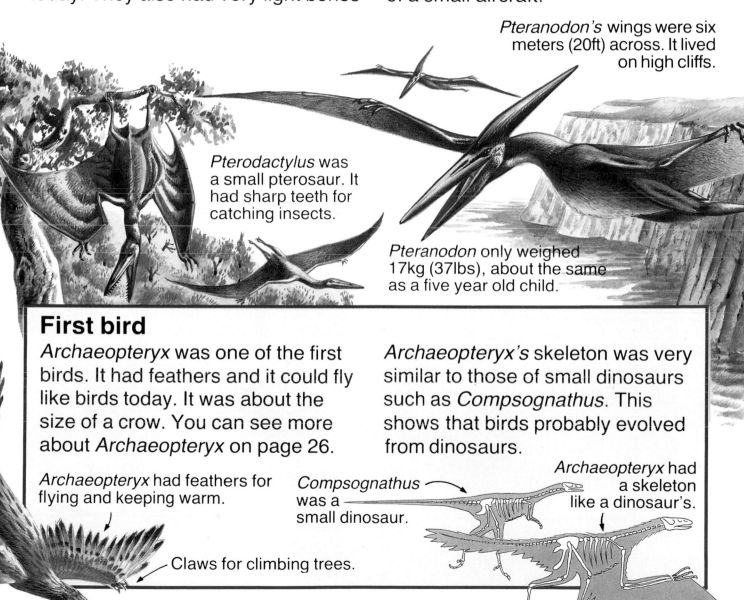

Pteranodon's wings were six meters (20ft) across. It lived on high cliffs.

Pterodactylus was a small pterosaur. It had sharp teeth for catching insects.

Pteranodon only weighed 17kg (37lbs), about the same as a five year old child.

First bird

Archaeopteryx was one of the first birds. It had feathers and it could fly like birds today. It was about the size of a crow. You can see more about *Archaeopteryx* on page 26.

Archaeopteryx's skeleton was very similar to those of small dinosaurs such as *Compsognathus*. This shows that birds probably evolved from dinosaurs.

Archaeopteryx had feathers for flying and keeping warm.

Compsognathus was a small dinosaur.

Archaeopteryx had a skeleton like a dinosaur's.

Claws for climbing trees.

13

Why did they die?

Experts know when dinosaurs died out but they are still not sure why. There are different ideas about what might have happened. Now scientists know many of these ideas are wrong.

Finding out from rocks

Fossil dinosaurs are found in rocks from the Mesozoic Era. But there are none in rocks that are newer than this.

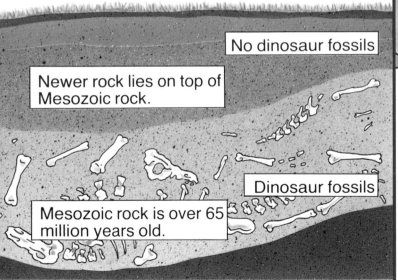

No dinosaur fossils

Newer rock lies on top of Mesozoic rock.

Dinosaur fossils

Mesozoic rock is over 65 million years old.

This shows that dinosaurs all became extinct 65 million years ago, at the end of the Mesozoic Era.

Too big?

Some scientists thought dinosaurs grew so huge that they could not support their own weight.

Now experts know that big dinosaurs had very strong skeletons.

Small dinosaurs became extinct too. So size cannot explain why they all died out.

Dying of diseases?

Some scientists thought diseases made dinosaurs extinct.

Some dinosaurs did have diseases, but they evolved to survive these. Now experts know that disease on its own can never make a type of animal extinct.

Beaten by mammals?

During the Mesozoic Era, a new kind of creature called mammals evolved. (You can read more about them later.)

Some experts thought mammals ate all the dinosaurs' food.

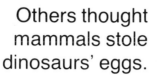

Others thought mammals stole dinosaurs' eggs.

Now scientists are sure that mammals did not make dinosaurs extinct. Mammals only became important after dinosaurs died out.

Poisonous flowers?

The first flowering plants evolved during the Cretaceous Period. Some experts thought they had chemicals that poisoned dinosaurs.

Now scientists know that new kinds of dinosaurs evolved especially to eat the new plants.

End of the line

During the Mesozoic Era, new dinosaurs always evolved to take the place of others. But at the end of the Era, dinosaurs all died out together, and no more evolved to replace them.

Something must have happened that killed all the dinosaurs and stopped new ones from evolving. The next four pages tell you more about this.

15

Big changes

The environment changed in many different ways while dinosaurs lived on Earth. Scientists think this might explain why dinosaurs died out.

Changes in plants

Many different kinds of plants evolved during the Mesozoic Era.

These plants lived during the Triassic and Jurassic Periods.

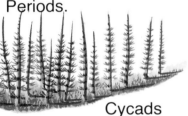

Cycads

Horsetails

These plants lived during the Cretaceous Period.

Flowering plants

Hardwood trees

Changes in plants meant dinosaurs' food was always changing too. But these changes were so gradual that dinosaurs could evolve to keep up.

Changes in the weather

The climate is the kind of weather that any place usually has.

Earth had a warm climate for most of the Mesozoic Era.

But at the end of the Cretaceous Period it became cooler. Experts think that cold weather helped to make dinosaurs extinct.

Dinosaurs had no fur or feathers to help store their body heat. Most of them were too big to warm up again after a long, cold winter.

Changes in the Earth's surface

The Earth's surface is broken into large pieces called plates. These move around so that the continents are always slowly changing position. This is called continental drift.

As the plates move, the Earth's environment and climate change. Some experts think this made dinosaurs extinct. These maps show how the Earth has changed.

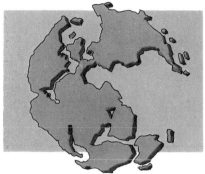

During the Triassic Period, there was just one big continent called Pangaea. The climate was warm all around the world.

During the Cretaceous Period, Pangaea split up into new continents and oceans were left in between them. Earth's climate became cooler.

This is what the Earth looks like today. The continents are still moving, but it happens too slowly for you to tell.

In the sea

As the land changed, so did the sea. Some experts think this killed millions of tiny sea creatures called Foraminifera, and other animals that ate them.

Foraminifera and many other sea creatures died out with dinosaurs.

Too slow

Continental drift takes a very long time. On its own, it does not explain why dinosaurs and other creatures all died out so suddenly.

A sudden change

Now scientists think dinosaurs died out because something violent suddenly changed the Earth's climate. Here is what may have happened.

What broke the food web?

Many scientists think a big lump of rock from outer space, called an asteroid, struck the Earth at the end of the Mesozoic Era.

The asteroid was probably 10 to 15 km (6 to 9 miles) across.

Nothing left to eat

All living things in any environment depend upon each other for their food. This is called a food web.

Caterpillars eat leaves

Shrews eat caterpillars

Owls eat shrews

If the dinosaurs' food web broke at the end of the Mesozoic Era, they would have died out. Here you can see why.

No plants

Plant eaters died

Meat eaters died

Where it landed

There are clues that an asteroid hit what is now Yucatan in Mexico.

The asteroid landed here.

Yucatan

Mexico

Experts have found tiny glass beads like this around the area. They are made of rock that melted when the asteroid struck the earth.

No sunlight

All living things close to where the asteroid struck were killed. Dust and gases filled the air all round the world. Sunlight was blocked out and the world became cold and dark.

Without sunlight, all the plants died.

When plants died, the food web broke down. This killed dinosaurs, and they soon became extinct.

How plants grow

You can see how plants need sunlight. Put some damp paper towel on a saucer and scatter cress seeds on it.

Leave the saucer in sunlight so the seeds can grow.

Cover some shoots with an egg cup.

Take the egg cup off after a week. The shoots without any sunlight will have died.

Volcanoes

65 million years ago there were also some huge volcanic eruptions in what is now India. These might have caused as much damage as an asteroid.

Some experts think dust and gases from these volcanoes might have blocked out the sunlight too.

Too hot?

When the asteroid struck, it threw up water vapor as well as dust. After the dust settled, water vapor stayed in the air. It trapped the heat of the sun, so the Earth heated up like a giant greenhouse.

Just as dinosaurs would have been killed by cold, they also would have died if it was too hot.

After dinosaurs

Not everything became extinct at the end of the Mesozoic Era. Plants grew up from seeds that had survived, and soon other animals began to fill the places left by dinosaurs.

More birds evolved to live in the air.

Small mammals lived in the trees and forests.

Some reptiles, such as crocodiles and turtles, still lived in fresh water.

About mammals

Mammals are animals that can keep their bodies warm all the time. Most mammals have fur or hair and do not lay eggs. They give birth to babies and feed them on milk.

Purgatorius lived 70 million years ago when dinosaurs were still around. It probably slept during the day, and came out at night. All later mammals evolved from animals like this.

Purgatorius was the size of a rat. It ate insects, and came out at night when dinosaurs were asleep.

Staying alive

Mammals' warm bodies helped them to survive when the climate changed and dinosaurs died out. They were also small enough to burrow holes and escape from the cold or heat.

Different kinds of mammal

The time since dinosaurs died out is called the Cenozoic Era. Many different mammals have evolved and died out during this time. Here you can see some that are now extinct.

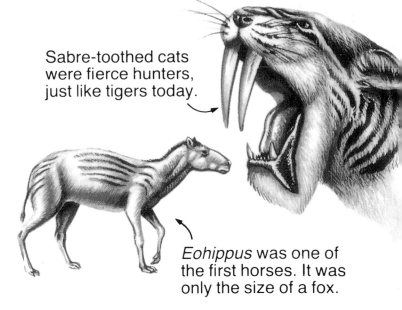

Sabre-toothed cats were fierce hunters, just like tigers today.

Paraceratherium was the largest ever land mammal. It was 8m (26ft) tall. That's six times as high as a man.

Eohippus was one of the first horses. It was only the size of a fox.

Dinosaur relatives

Tuataras lived over 150 million years ago, at the same time as dinosaurs. Some still live in New Zealand today.

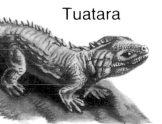

Tuatara

Chaffinch

Modern birds evolved from prehistoric birds like *Archaeopteryx,* and they still have very similar skeletons to dinosaurs. This shows that birds are dinosaurs' closest relatives today.

Out of the trees

People are mammals. Most experts think we evolved from creatures like apes that lived in the trees about 10 million years ago.

The first people were hunters who could walk upright on two legs. They learned how to use tools, build shelters and make fire.

21

Today

Since dinosaurs died out, many other living things have become extinct. Today most extinctions are caused by the things people do.

Damage to wildlife

Wildlife means all the wild plants and animals living in the world. The main danger to wildlife comes from people damaging or changing the environment where it lives.

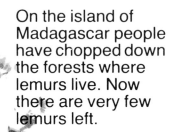

On the island of Madagascar people have chopped down the forests where lemurs live. Now there are very few lemurs left.

Pollution is waste left by people, such as garbage or poisonous chemicals. Pollution in the environment harms everything that lives there.

Oil spilled in the sea kills many sea birds, such as cormorants.

Hunting

If animals are hunted too much, they can become extinct. People hunt animals for many different reasons.

Ocelots and other wild cats are hunted just for their beautiful skins. Now they are becoming very rare.

People make ocelot skins into fur coats.

Dodos were once hunted for food. They became extinct 300 years ago.

Living together

It is important to look after the environment and protect wildlife. All living things are connected to each other by food webs. If one thing disappears, many others may suffer.

For example, snakes eat rats. In parts of Africa, people killed lots of snakes. Soon there were too many rats. They began to eat people's crops, so people suffered.

Safe places

There are many ways to help wildlife. People can stop hunting animals and protect the places where they live.

Over 15 thousand elephants live in Hwange wildlife park in Africa. Here they are safe from hunters.

How to help

There are lots of things you can do to help protect your environment. Here are some ideas.

Always put your garbage in a trash can.

Never damage plants or pick wild flowers.

Try not to waste things. Reuse plastic bags and take glass bottles to a bottle return if you can.

You could join a conservation group near your home. They organize lots of activities. You can find out about them at your nearest library.

Keep watch

Today you can only see dinosaurs in museums. But you can still see many other fascinating creatures living on Earth. It is up to everyone to stop them from disappearing as dinosaurs did.

Where to see dinosaurs

Dinosaur fossils have been discovered all over the world. In most countries you can visit places to see dinosaurs and find out more about them.

Stuck in the rock

At the Dinosaur National Monument in Utah, U.S.A., there is a cliff full of dinosaur bones. Here you can see the remains of giants such as *Diplodocus*, *Apatasaurus* and *Stegosaurus*.

Biggest bones

The world's largest dinosaur skeleton is a *Brachiosaurus* from East Africa, which you can see at the Berlin Natural History Museum in Germany.

A recent find

In London's Natural History Museum you can see lots of dinosaurs and other fossils. They include the fish-eating dinosaur *Baryonyx*, which was discovered in England in 1986.

Giant steps

At Peace River Canyon in Canada, you can see lots of fossil footprints. These show where dinosaurs walked across the river bed millions of years ago.

Eggs from the desert

Hundreds of fossil *Protoceratops* eggs have been found in the Gobi desert in Mongolia. You can see them at the Academy of Sciences in Ulan Bator.

There is probably a place near you where you can see dinosaurs and other fossils. You can find out about museums at your local library.

HOW DOES A BIRD FLY?

Kate Woodward

Designed by Mary Forster
Illustrated by Isabel Bowring

Consultant: Robin Horner (Warden, RSPB)

CONTENTS

Additional illustrations by Joseph McEwan and Guy Smith

Early fliers

Some of the creatures that lived on Earth over 200 million years ago, at the same time as the dinosaurs, could fly. They were called pterosaurs.

Pterosaurs had wings made of leathery skin, not feathers. For this reason, scientists do not count them as birds.

pterosaur

Some pterosaurs had wings about 7m (almost 26ft) across. That's nearly as long as a bus.

Pterosaurs had jaws like beaks.

Compsognathus

None of the dinosaurs could fly.

The first bird

The first animal that scientists call a bird is the Archaeopteryx. It lived about 140 million years ago. They think it developed from dinosaurs that could not fly, not from pterosaurs.

It was about the size of a crow and had feathers on its body and wings.

Archaeopteryx

Odd bird

This Hoatzin chick is similar to the earliest known birds. It has unusual claws on its wings, like an Archaeopteryx (see below). It lives in the forests of South America today.

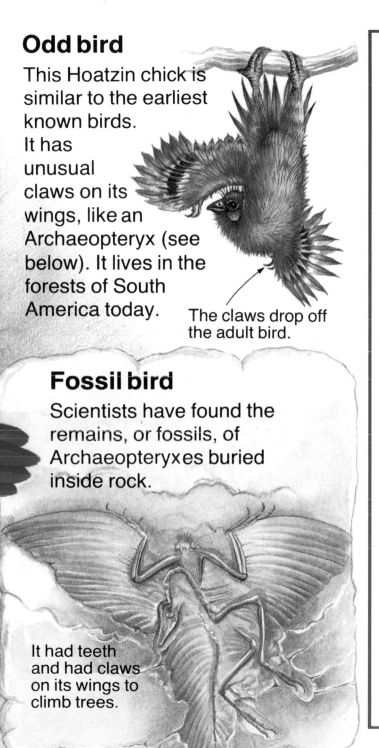

The claws drop off the adult bird.

Fossil bird

Scientists have found the remains, or fossils, of Archaeopteryxes buried inside rock.

It had teeth and had claws on its wings to climb trees.

All kinds of birds

There are more than 8,650 kinds of birds in the world today and they are all very different. They live in places as cold as the North Pole and as hot as the tropical rainforests around the Equator.

Ostriches live on the grasslands in Africa. They cannot fly, but can run very fast.

ostrich

budgie

Budgerigars are popular pets. Wild budgies live in large groups, or flocks, in Australia.

Geese live near water. Their young are called goslings.

goose and gosling

penguin

Some penguins live in the Antarctic near the South Pole. They are very good swimmers, but cannot fly.

A bird's body

To help birds to fly, their bodies are very light and streamlined. This means they are a smooth shape so they slip through the air easily. Here you can see the parts of a bird's body.

Wings

Birds have wings instead of arms. They are strong and light enough to make a bird fly when it flaps them.

Feathers are made of keratin, like our hair.

Feathers

Birds are the only animals with feathers. Small birds have about 1,000 feathers. Large birds can have as many as 25,000.

Eggs in a nest

All birds lay eggs. They do this so they do not have to carry their young around inside them before they are born.

Eyes

Many birds have eyes on opposite sides of their head so they can see as much around them as possible.

chick

This beak is good for catching fish.

Beak

Birds have different shaped beaks depending on what food they eat.

Neck

Birds have very limber necks. They can turn their heads around to point backward to clean themselves with their beaks.

Ears

A bird's ears are hard to see. But they can hear very quiet sounds.

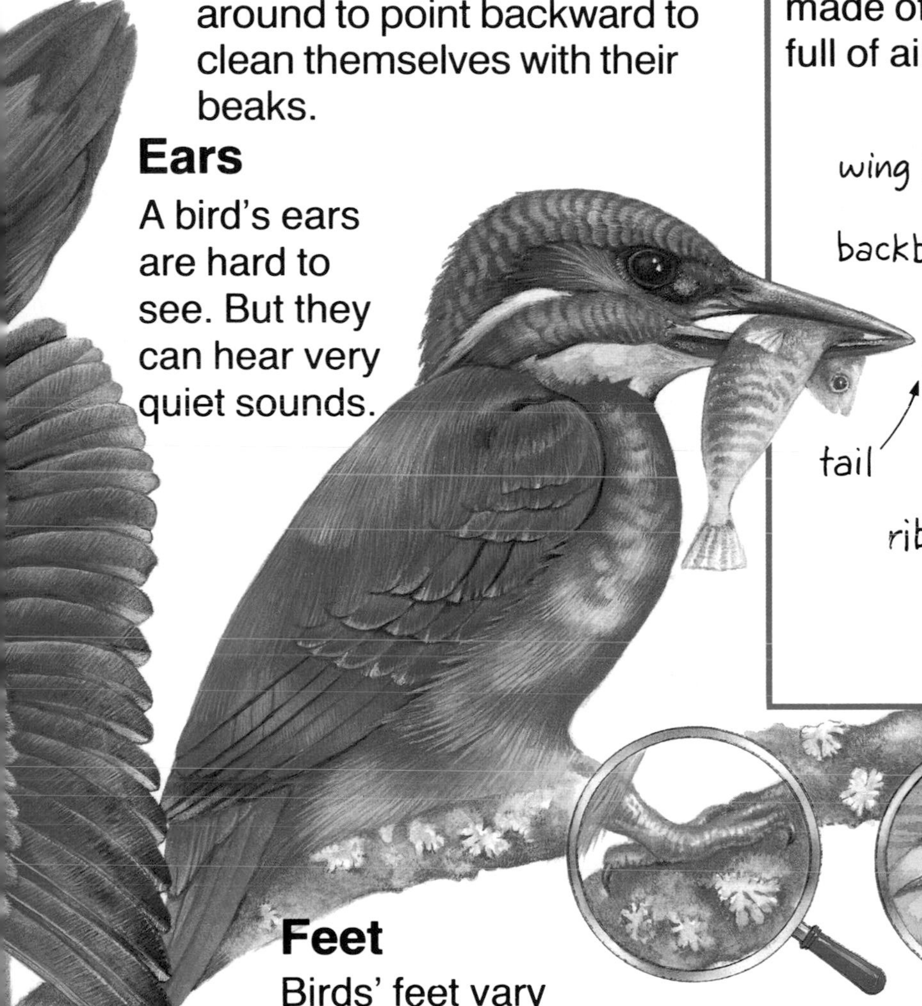

Inside a bird

If a bird is too heavy it cannot fly. To make it lighter, its skeleton is made of hollow bones. These are full of air.

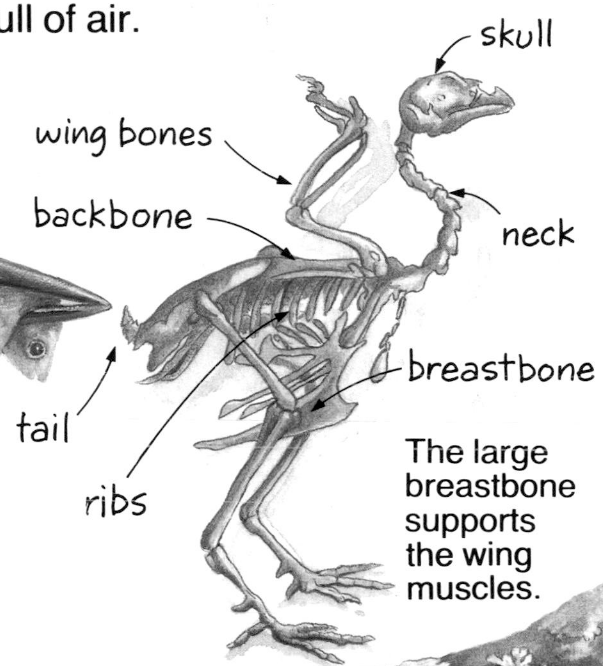

skull

wing bones

backbone

neck

tail

breastbone

ribs

The large breastbone supports the wing muscles.

Feet

Birds' feet vary in shape and size. Many use their toes to grip branches.

A kingfisher's feet are covered in scaly skin.

A lily trotter has very long toes to walk over soft mud.

A goose has webbed feet which it uses for paddling.

29

Feathers

Feathers keep birds warm, stop their bodies from getting wet and help them to fly. All birds have different types of feathers. You can see them on this drake (male duck).

Down feathers

Down feathers are the very soft ones next to the bird's skin. They help keep the bird warm.

Tail feathers

Birds use their tail feathers to steer themselves in the air and to balance on the ground.

A woodpecker uses its tail to hold itself steady against a tree.

Wing feathers

The long feathers on the wings are the most important in helping the bird to fly.

The feathers on a bird's body are called its plumage.

wing feathers

tail feathers

mallard

body feathers

Body feathers

Body feathers lie smoothly over the down feathers. They are oily so that they are waterproof. This stops the bird getting cold and wet.

Moulting

Adult birds lose old feathers a few at a time and grow new ones. This is called moulting.

Cleaning and preening

Birds spend a lot of time looking after their feathers to keep them clean and healthy. They pull each feather through the tip of their beak. This is called preening.

scarlet macaw

Preening gets rid of tiny insects, such as lice, which like to live in feathers.

Feather color

Some birds have bright feathers so they get noticed. This helps them attract a mate. lorikeet

Others have feathers the same color as the things around them, so they are hard to see and can hide from enemies. grouse

A flamingo has pink feathers. This color comes from the food it eats. flamingo

Taking a bath

You can often see small birds bathing in water or in dust.

A bird gets dirt and lice off its feathers by rubbing itself in dust.

Make your own birdbath

Small birds like to splash in water. You can make a birdbath in your garden using an upturned old trash can lid filled with water.

Borrow a bird book from your library to help you recognise birds that come to use it.

Built to fly

Three types of animals can fly – birds, bats and insects. Birds are the best fliers because of the shape of their wings.

Not a bird

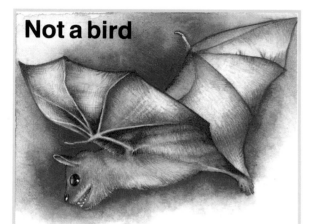

A bat is not a bird as it has no feathers. Its body is furry and it has leathery skin on its wings. It belongs to the type of animals called mammals.

Birdmen

In the past, men tried to fly like birds. They made wings and fixed them to their arms, but were too heavy to fly.

The wing

A bird's wing is a special shape, rounded on top and curved underneath. This is called an airfoil and helps lift the bird as it flaps its wings.

In flight, air passes smoothly over the wing.

airfoil shape

golden eagle

primary flight feathers

Primary means "first". The long primary feathers are the main ones that power the bird through the air.

secondary flight feathers

The secondary flight feathers help make the airfoil shape.

wing coverts

The wing coverts help make the wing rounded on top.

In flight

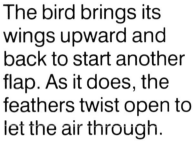

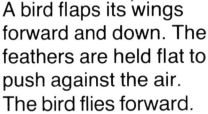

A bird flaps its wings forward and down. The feathers are held flat to push against the air. The bird flies forward.

The bird brings its wings upward and back to start another flap. As it does, the feathers twist open to let the air through.

To change direction or go up and down, the bird tilts its body to one side and moves its wings or tail to steer through the air.

Make your own airfoil

1

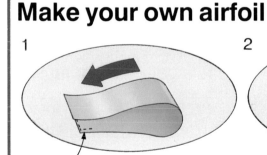

glue here

2

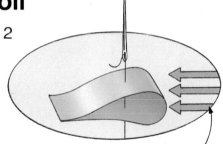

blow hard here

air on top presses less

3

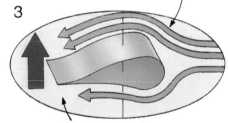

air below pushes up

1. Bend a long piece of paper into an airfoil shape. Glue the ends together and a little way up the side edges as shown.

2. Using a needle, thread cotton through the middle of the paper*. Blow hard over the curved end of the paper. What happens?

3. Air rushes fast over the top of the airfoil. This air presses less against the airfoil than the air below, so the airfoil rises up.

*Get an adult to help you.

Different ways to fly

The shape of a bird's wing tells you something about how it flies. Next to the birds on these pages is a small picture of their wing shapes to help you recognise them.

Speedy swallows

A swallow has curved, pointed wings. This good airfoil shape makes the air rush fast over the top of them. Swallows flap their wings very fast to speed along.

It tucks its short legs into its body while it is flying so they do not slow it down.

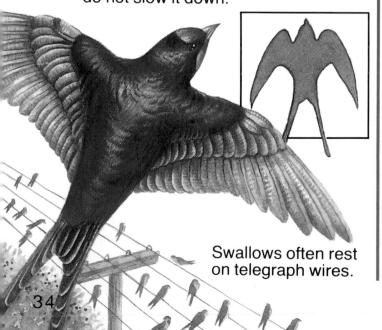

Swallows often rest on telegraph wires.

Fastest bird

The peregrine falcon is a bird of prey. This means that it hunts other small birds and animals.

When it hunts, it circles high in the sky looking for prey.

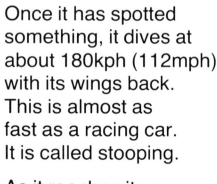

Once it has spotted something, it dives at about 180kph (112mph) with its wings back. This is almost as fast as a racing car. It is called stooping.

As it reaches its prey, the falcon swings its feet forwards and knocks the victim with its claws.

Long distance fliers

Many geese, such as these snow geese, fly very long distances to where they nest. They fly for many hours without stopping and have long, broad wings which they do not need to flap very fast.

Geese often make a 'honking' noise as they fly.

Straight from the nest

Once a chick is strong enough it flies straight from its nest. At first, it makes short, practice flights from bush to bush.

A mother tempts her chicks out of the nest with food.

Short flights

A jay has wide, blunt wings which it flaps slowly. This makes it easy to twist and turn through trees.

Birds with wings this shape usually only fly for short distances.

35

Flying with the wind

Many birds use the wind to help them stay up in the air. Some keep their wings still and let the wind carry them along. Others beat their wings against the air to stay in one spot.

Riding on air

Many large birds stay in the air for a long time without flapping their wings. This is called gliding.

An albatross hardly flaps its wings at all. It can fly like this for days just using the wind.

An albatross has very long, narrow wings for fast gliding over the sea.

It spends most of its life out at sea and is rarely seen, except by sailors.

Gliding over the sea

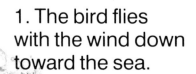
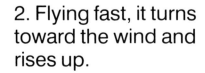

wind

1. The bird flies with the wind down toward the sea.

2. Flying fast, it turns toward the wind and rises up.

3. Then it turns and flies fast with the wind again.

High fliers

When the sun heats the ground, warm air spirals upward. These drafts of warm air are called thermals. Most large birds of prey use their long wings to soar upward on thermals.

Once it is at the top of a thermal it glides down to reach another.

thermal

The bird is carried up high by the rising warm air. It does not need to flap its wings.

Vultures can soar for many hours at a time without becoming exhausted.

Staying in one spot

Many birds beat their wings fast against the air to stay in one spot. This is called hovering. A hummingbird hovers to feed.

It beats its wings in a figure of eight shape nearly 50 times every second.

Bird spotting

Try to recognise everyday birds by their wing shape. Draw them, then check in a guide to see what type they are.

Going up and coming down

Birds may live in trees, on water or on cliff tops so they take-off and land in different ways. Most take off by springing into the air.

Running take-off

Large birds are too heavy to spring up. This coot has to run fast for a long way, splashing across the water, before it gets up in the air.

It stretches its neck out to make itself more streamlined.

Using sea breezes

Cormorants nest on cliff tops where there are strong sea breezes. They jump off cliffs with their wings open so the wind lifts them up.

Cormorants live in large groups called colonies.

Lazy flier

Pheasants do not like flying much. But if they are frightened they flap their broad wings and take off almost straight up in the air.

Their wings are short so they do not hit branches and trees.

Landing on a branch

All birds have to slow down before they can land safely.

As a bullfinch comes in to land it spreads its tail feathers out like a fan.

The feathers act like a brake and slow down the bird's flight.

It brings its feet forward ready to land.

It flaps its wings back and forth to slow it down more.

Landing on water

A swan is one of the heaviest flying birds.

Swans land on water. They put their large webbed feet down first and push against the water. This slows them down before they land. They look as if they are water-skiing.

Its toes grip tight around the branch as it lands, so it does not fall off.

As it settles, the bird closes its tail feathers and tucks in its wings.

39

Migration

Many kinds of birds fly from one part of the world to another every year. This is called migration. They make this long journey to a warmer place where there is plenty of food.

Birds on the moon

In the past people did not know where birds spent the winter. Some thought that they flew to the moon.

BRITISH ISLES

EUROPE

ATLANTIC OCEAN

SAHARA DESERT

Following stars

Birds find their way by watching the sun during the day and following the stars by night. Something inside them acts like a clock. It tells them when to set off.

Before the journey

Before they set off, birds eat plenty of food to store up energy for their journey.

BRAZIL

SOUTH AMERICA

The shear-water's journey takes less than 20 days.

Over oceans

Manx shearwaters migrate across the Atlantic Ocean to the coast of Brazil. They return to northern Europe once the weather is warmer there.

Bad weather

During bad weather, when the sun is hidden by clouds, birds can lose their way.

One goose leads and the others follow in a "V" pattern.

Out of the Arctic

Whooper swans nest in Siberia in the Arctic Circle. In winter many fly to north-west Europe.

Over mountains

Bar-headed geese fly over the Himalaya mountains at over 8,000m (26,000ft), as high as a jet plane.

HIMALAYAS

INDIA

ARABIAN SEA

AFRICA

Studying birds

Sometimes migrating birds are shot for sport. Ornithologists (people who study birds) count the birds to see if there are fewer of one type. Then they try and protect them from hunters.

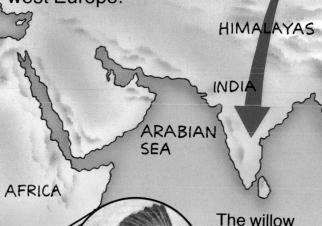

The willow warbler flies non-stop for four days and nights to cross the desert.

Over deserts

The tiny willow warbler flies more than 4,000km (2,400 miles) from Europe across the Sahara Desert to Africa.

Be an ornithologist

Look out for migrating birds gathering on telegraph wires before they leave in autumn. Find out which birds arrive in spring to tell you warm weather is coming.

Night owls

Most owls do not fly about much during the day. This is because they are roosting, or sleeping. They come out at night to hunt.

Night hunters

Owls are good at hunting at night. Their wings, eyes and ears are specially made to make flying and hunting in the dark easier.

A tawny owl has shorter wings than some other owls, for flying among trees.

Owls have huge eyes. Some are almost as big as human eyes.

tawny owl

facial disc

Their ears are behind the face feathers, called the facial disc, at the side of their head.

Owls have sharp, hooked beaks for carrying and tearing up their food.

soft fringes

These sharp claws, called talons, are for catching and killing food.

An owl has soft fringes on the edge of its wing feathers. These help it fly almost silently, so that small animals do not hear it coming.

Protecting our owls

Some owls lose their homes and hunting grounds when farmers cut down trees to make fields. You can find out which owls are threatened and how to help by joining a local bird club. Your library will help you find one.

Hunting for food

A barn owl is a very agile flier. It has large, broad wings which it flaps slowly. It can take-off vertically, stop suddenly in mid-flight and hover in one spot. It needs to do all these to hunt well.

The owl glides silently through the air listening for sounds and watching the ground.

barn owl

When he hears a mouse, he flies overhead and hovers for a moment. Then he pounces.

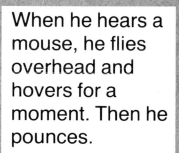

Waiting for supper

Before they can fly, the young owls wait at the nest for their parents to bring food.

At the last moment, he swings his sharp talons forward to catch the mouse.

43

Birds that cannot fly

There are a few birds that cannot fly. Some have found different ways to get around such as swimming or running, so they no longer need to fly.

Champion swimmers

Penguins cannot fly because their wings have become more like flippers. They use them to swim.

Birds of the past

The giant elephant bird once lived on Madagascar and the dodo on Mauritius, both islands off Africa.

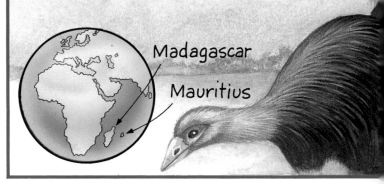

Madagascar

Mauritius

Their flippers are short and thin, like paddles. They are good for pushing themselves along underwater.

Penguins have a very thick layer of tightly-packed feathers covering their bodies to help keep them warm in the frozen Antarctic.

emperor penguin

They swim near the surface of the water and dive down to catch fish.

When people went to live there, they hunted the birds and stole their eggs. Soon there were no birds left.

dodo

They could not fly to safety as they had such tiny wings.

elephant bird

Flightless cormorants

Cormorants living on the Galapagos Islands have no enemies. They have lost the ability to fly because they do not need to.

They have plenty of food to eat from the seas around the islands.

Adélie penguins often march one after the other, "following the leader", across the snow.

adélie penguin

They waddle as they walk, using their flippers to balance.

Too heavy to fly

An ostrich is about 2.5m (8ft) tall and weighs 150kg (330lbs), nearly as much as two adults. It can't fly, but runs very fast.

Its ancestors could not fly.

Birds which weigh more than 15-20kg (30-45lbs) are too heavy to fly.

45

Amazing fliers

On this page you can find out about some amazing flying feats.

Non-stop flier

Swifts can fly for up to three years non-stop. They eat, drink, bathe and sleep as they fly.

One swift lived for 16 years and could have flown up to eight million km (nearly five million miles). This equals about 200 times around the world.

Biggest flying bird

The Andean condor is the biggest flying bird in the world. Its wings spread out from tip to tip are 3.2m (nearly 11ft). It uses them to glide in thermal currents.

Its wings are nearly four times the length of your arms outstretched.

The greatest traveller

The Arctic tern makes the longest migration of all birds. Each year it flies from the Arctic Circle to the Antarctic and back again, to spend the summer at each Pole in turn.

North Pole

At each Pole there is sunshine for 24 hours a day during the summer.

swift

So these terns see more daylight than any other bird in the world.

Arctic tern

South Pole

Smallest bird

The bee hummingbird from Cuba is the smallest bird in the world. It is only 57mm (2¼ inches) from beak to tail. This is about as long as your thumb.

The hummingbird gets its name from the noise its wings make as it hovers.

46

Rarest of all

Although there are lots of birds, some are becoming rare. Like the dodo they could die out unless we look after them and protect their homes.

Shot to extinction

There were once thousands of passenger pigeons in America.

None of these pigeons is alive today because they were all shot down and killed for sport.

Secret nests

Not long ago there were only a few ospreys living in Britain. Their nests had to be kept secret so no-one could steal their eggs.

Never steal eggs from a bird's nest.

Birds of the rainforest

Every day, large areas of rainforests are chopped down and burned. The birds who live there are in danger of dying out because they are losing their homes.

hyacinth macaw

toucan

hummingbird

Andean cock of the rock

rosella

Bird puzzle

Can you identify these different birds by their shape? They are all in this part of the book.

Find them and learn their names. The answers are at the bottom of this page.

1.

2.

3.

4.

5.

6.

7.

8.

9.

10.

48

HOW DO ANIMALS TALK?

Susan Mayes

Designed by Claire Littlejohn, Brian Robertson and Mary Forster

Illustrated by Angela Hargreaves, Philip Hood and Colin King

Consultant: Joyce Pope

CONTENTS

Ways of talking

People talk to each other for all kinds of reasons. They talk using words, but they also say things in other ways. Different movements, sounds and faces all help you say what you mean.

This face shows sadness.

A "shhh" sound helps say "be quiet".

You may greet your best friend by stretching out your arms to them.

Life in the wild

In the wild, animals must "talk" to each other so that they can survive and bring up their families. For example, you can see how important this is for your cat's wild relative, the lion.

A lioness's special scent tells males when she is ready to mate.

lioness

Watching your pets

Animals say things to each other all the time. They don't use words, of course, but they do "talk" in other ways, just as we do. Try watching your pets to see what they do.

You may see your dog bow to another dog like this. He is saying "play with me". He may do this to you too.

If your dog pokes another one in the side with his nose, he is saying "stand still".

50

The parents and their babies must understand each other so the family can keep safely together.

Lionesses teach their cubs to hunt and to protect themselves.

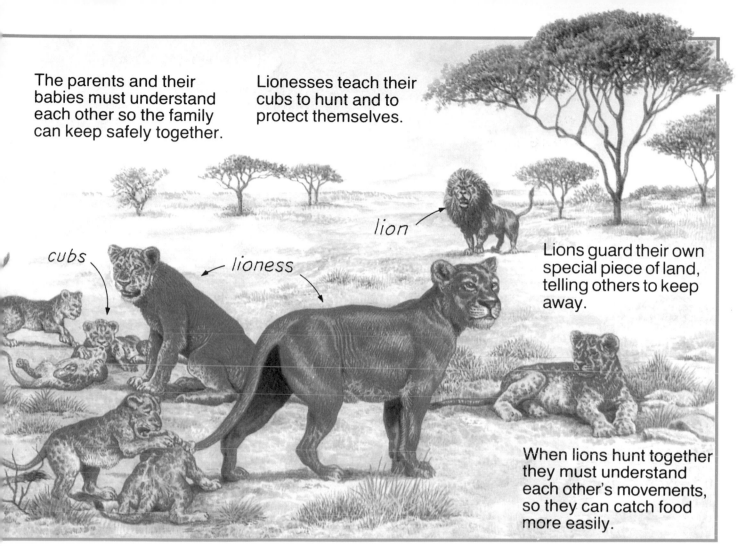

cubs

lioness

lion

Lions guard their own special piece of land, telling others to keep away.

When lions hunt together they must understand each other's movements, so they can catch food more easily.

If you have pet cats you will often see them rubbing noses like this in a friendly greeting.

Animals "talk" to each other with many movements, sounds and smells. Some have special colors and patterns.

These all make clear messages which are full of important information for family, friends and even enemies.

Saying "keep out"

The place where an animal finds food, water and a mate is very important. The animal guards part of it, to keep away others of its own kind.

The part the animals guard is called its territory. Territory owners must make clear warnings which tell others "keep out, I live here".

Making a noise

Many animals make sounds to warn others "this is my territory". Noises are a good warning because they travel a long way.

Birds such as gulls make a simple call which says "this is mine". Other birds, such as this thrush, sing complicated songs.

Each kind of bird has a different song. Usually, the male sings it. He learns the song by listening to the adult males when he is young.

When the bird is ready to guard territory of his own, he adds new parts to his song. This makes a stronger "keep out" signal.

A bird's song is usually meant for birds of his own kind. This thrush is singing to warn other thrushes nearby.

This thrush recognizes his neighbor's song and will keep out of his territory.

Rat-a-tat-tat

A male woodpecker marks his territory with a loud rat-a-tat-tat. He makes the sound by drumming his beak on a hollow branch or tree.

The woodpecker in this picture makes about 25 drums a second. When he is feeding he only makes a short tap-tap.

The lion's roar

Lions live in groups called prides. A pride's territory can be up to twenty kilometers (around twelve miles) across.

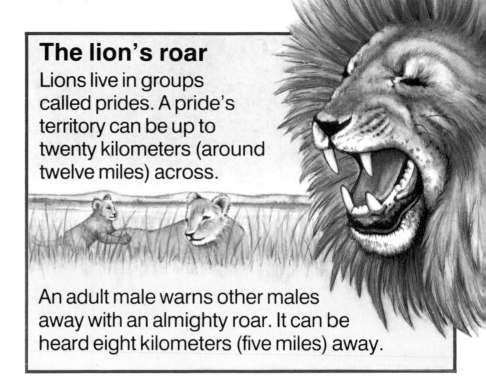

An adult male warns other males away with an almighty roar. It can be heard eight kilometers (five miles) away.

Noises underwater

The male haddock guards his underwater territory by making noises. He moves special muscles so they drum against a part called his swim bladder.

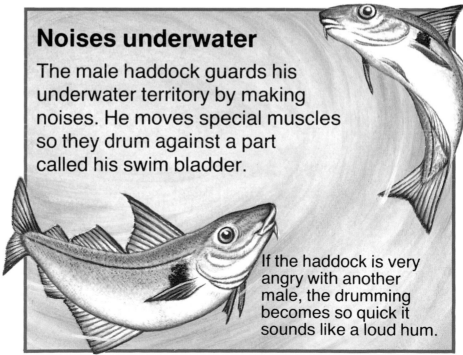

If the haddock is very angry with another male, the drumming becomes so quick it sounds like a loud hum.

More warnings

Different animals have different ways of saying "keep out of my territory". Bright colors, claw marks and strong smells are all warnings to strangers.

Some animals make themselves look bigger than they really are.

You may have seen a cat puff out its hair if a strange cat comes into the garden. This is called a display.

Warning color

When a male stickleback fish is ready to build his nest and look for a mate, his tummy turns bright red.

If he sees the red tummy of another male in his territory he gets very angry and chases the fish away.

The Australian frilled lizard raises its bright neck flap and opens its mouth wide if an enemy comes too close.

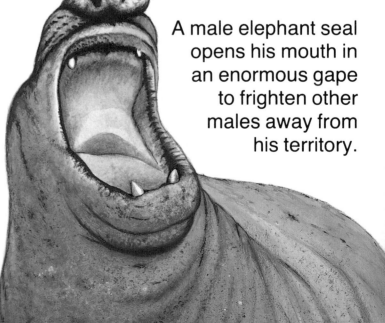

A male elephant seal opens his mouth in an enormous gape to frighten other males away from his territory.

Smelly messages

Many animals have a very good sense of smell and they mark their territories with smelly messages.

An otter marks its own special exit from the water by leaving droppings on a stone.

The scent of a dropping can las for many weeks.

Dogs mark places where they live and walk by urinating. First, they sniff to smell who else has been there.

Stink fights

Male ring-tailed lemurs have stink fights to win territory. Their smelly scent is made under the skin of their arms.

Each lemur pulls his tail between his arms, then he waves it about. The one with the strongest scent usually wins.

"I was here"

Bears mark their territory by scratching at trees. The claw marks warn other bears "I was here".

55

Finding a mate

Most kinds of animals look for a mate each year, so they can have babies.

The meeting place

Every year Uganda kobs meet at a place called a lek. The males gather to fight for small pieces of territory. A female visits a male's territory when she is ready to find a mate.

Usually, a male makes signals to a female, inviting her to be his partner.

These male kobs are fighting for territory. The weaker animal will give in.

This male is displaying to a female who has come into his territory. He is showing off by dancing near her, to see if she will be his partner.

Beautiful birds

Male birds are usually more colorful than the females. They use their brightly colored feathers to make beautiful displays to the female birds.

A male blue bird of paradise hangs upside down and fans out his blue and green feathers.

Calling out

Many male animals tell females where they are by calling out to them. Male frogs call to the females by making loud croaking noises.

This frog's croak sounds loud because it echoes inside his puffed out pouch.

A male bush cricket calls to a female by rubbing his wings together.

Smelling the air

Some animals, like this male gypsy moth, can smell a mate from far away. The moth's big antenna help him smell a female moth's special scent.

A male golden pheasant circles his mate. He opens a feathery fan on the side of his head which is closest to her.

A peacock stands in front of the female, the peahen, and displays to her by shaking his enormous curved feathers.

Family talk

Animal parents and their babies must talk to each other for many reasons. They need to know how to recognize each other, so the family can stay safely together. They must also understand each other when they feed.

A voice from the egg

Some baby animals talk with their mother even before they are born.

Chicks make cheeping noises while they are still in the shell and the hen answers.

A female Nile crocodile buries her eggs in the sand. When the babies are ready to hatch they make a peeping call. The mother hears the noise and uncovers the eggs, so the babies can get out.

"Are you my mother?"

Many baby animals learn to recognize their parents almost as soon as they are born. This is called imprinting.

When birds hatch, their parents are usually the first things they see. These ducklings are following their mother.

Hungry chicks

Many kinds of chicks have brightly colored throats. This color is a signal to the parents. When they see it they feed their hungry babies.

In some birds, the parents have colorful signalling marks.

An adult gull has a bright spot on its bottom jaw. When a chick sees the color it taps the spot. This makes the parent bring up food which it has been storing specially inside its body.

Sometimes, the first thing a baby animal sees is not its real parent, but another animal.

These baby geese have never seen their real mother. They have imprinted on a dog and they follow it everywhere.

Important smells

Some animals recognize each other by smell. A female sheep learns the smell and taste of her lambs. She will not look after another mother's lamb.

This sheep can recognize the voice of her own lamb among the bleating of all the others.

Living together

Many animals spend their lives together, in a group. Here are some of the ways they say things to each other with their bodies and faces.

Chimpanzee language

Chimpanzees often talk using different movements, just as we do.

A chimp greets a more important member of the group by holding out its hand. The other one shows it is friendly by touching the hand.

Chimps sometimes show they are friendly by kissing when they meet.

Chimps calm each other by hugging and touching.

Making faces

Chimps make many different faces to say how they feel. They also add to their messages with different calls.

This chimp's smile shows that it is happy. Your smile says the same thing.

This chimp seems to be laughing, but it is not happy at all. It is frightened.

This hard stare means that the chimp is angry and may attack.

An angry gorilla

An adult male gorilla makes a frightening and noisy warning display if he feels threatened.

As part of the display the gorilla beats his chest. The loud booming sound can be heard far away.

Showing who is boss

In many groups each animal has a special place in order of importance. This is called the pecking order. Wolves in a pack signal with their faces and tails to show their position.

This is the pack ▶ leader. His ears stand up and point forward. He holds his tail higher than the others.

◀ When the leader is near, this less important wolf flattens his ears and drops his tail between his legs.

These wolves are fighting to be the pack leader. The loser rolls on to his back baring his throat to the winner.
▼

61

Looking for food

Some kinds of animals hunt and feed in groups. It is easier to find food when there are lots of pairs of eyes keeping a look-out.

It is also easier to spy danger. Here are some of the ways different animals say things to each other when they are looking for food.

African hunting dogs

Before a hunt, African hunting dogs get ready by licking and nudging each other. They soon get excited and set off together.

On the hunt, the dogs' strong scent helps them keep in contact. Their white-tipped tails help them to see each other.

Afterwards, the hunters will go back to their den to feed the puppies and dogs who stayed behind.

The hungry dogs ask for food by licking the hunters' lips. Then the hunters bring up bits of meat which they gobbled at the kill.

62

Smelly trails

A family of ants is called a colony. The worker ants search for food. They leave scent trails as they run along. When a worker ant finds plenty of food it takes some back to the nest.

Soon more workers leave the nest and find food by following the trail. They smell the scent with their antenna.

Worker ants are females. This one is tapping the ground with her antenna so she can smell where to go.

Feeding the flock

Different kinds of small songbirds sometimes gather in a flock to hunt for berries and seeds. They call to each other to say where there is food or to warn about enemies.

The birds make about 25 different sounds, each with a special meaning.

"Come and help"

Sometimes an ant finds a piece of food which is too big for it to carry, so it tells the others to "come and help". It does this by hitting them with its antenna and front legs.

Different kinds of ants eat different food. Some eat plants and some eat other creatures. These black ants eat both.

63

Busy bees

There can be as many as fifty thousand bees in a honeybee colony. Colonies are made up of three kinds of bees*.

The queen is the biggest and most important bee. Each hive has one queen. She lays eggs and is mother of all the bees.

The worker bees are females. They collect food, do the cleaning and feed the queen. They do not lay eggs.

The drone bees are males. They mate with a few special females who then become queens of new colonies.

The queen's scent

Bees crowd around the queen. They try to touch her and lick her.

The queen bee has a strong scent which has a powerful effect on the rest of the colony. As long as the queen is there the bees work calmly.

* See pages 97-120 for more on bees.

Strangers beware

Every bee colony has its own scent. Sometimes, a stranger from another colony tries to get into the hive, but the bees recognize its different scent and push it out.

The intruder curls up. This tells the other bees "I give in".

"Food is this way"

Honeybees visit flowers to collect pollen and sweet food called nectar. When a worker bee finds plenty of food, she tells the others where to find it by doing a special dance.

The round dance

If the food is nearby the dancer moves in a circle, going one way then the other way.

The bees touch her and copy her. They can smell the pollen on her fur, so they know which kind of flower to look for.

The waggle dance

If a bee finds food far away from the hive she dances in the shape of a squashed figure 8. In the straight part she waggles her body very quickly.

This waggling bit of the dance is called the waggle run.

The speed of the dance and the direction of the waggle run tell the bees how far away the food is. They also tell the bees which way to fly.

When the bees find the flowers they collect food. They will return to the hive and do the dance themselves.

Staying safe

Animals mostly say things to their own kind, but if they are in danger they say things to other creatures too. They even talk to their enemies.

Patterned warnings

Poisonous animals often have bright patterns which tell enemies "don't eat me, I'm dangerous". Attackers get a nasty shock if they ignore the warning. They soon learn to keep away.

This coral snake is very poisonous. Its red, yellow and black bands are a clear warning to other animals.

A wasp can give a nasty sting. Its yellow and black stripes are a bright "danger" warning.

If this sort of boxfish is frightened it gives off a poisonous slime. Its colorful pattern tells enemies that it is dangerous to come near.

A sudden surprise

Some animals escape from an attacker by surprising it. This moth looks the same color as the tree it is resting on, but its bright hind wings are hidden.

If the moth is disturbed, it flies and startles the attacker with a flash of color. Then it settles again. The attacker thinks the moth has gone.

"I'm watching you"

Some animals are born with a clever disguise. They have markings which look like big eyes. This trick message can frighten or confuse an enemy.

If the eyed hawk-moth is disturbed it moves its front wings to show two big spots underneath. They look like the eyes of a big animal.

The elephant hawk-moth caterpillar has large eye markings. These make the front of its body look like a snake's head.

Many kinds of butterfly fishes have a dark spot near the tail. This confuses enemies as they think they are looking at the head.

An early warning

When some birds sense danger they make a loud, frightened call. Other kinds of birds understand there is something wrong and join in.

If you hear lots of excited birdcalls in a garden, it may mean there is a cat around.

Talking underwater

Whales, dolphins and many kinds of fishes make sounds, movements or even special smells to say things in their underwater world. Sound is a strong signal as it travels well in water.

Dolphin language

Dolphins live in groups called schools. They say things with lots of noises including squawks, whistles, groans, burps and clicks.

Hawaiian spinner dolphins are most noisy in the evening, when they are about to go hunting.

When they all join in a special chorus of noises this means they are ready to leave.

The dolphins also leap and slap the water with their bodies. This helps show where everyone is before they go.

Whales

Whales call to each other with loud sounds which other whales can hear many kilometers away. They make high trumpeting noises and low grunting sounds.

Scientists think these noises may help the whales keep in touch with each other when they are far apart.

Mystery songs

Humpback whales make sounds which they repeat in long, complicated patterns. Scientists call these "songs", but nobody knows what the songs mean.

A humpback whale usually sings when it is looking for a mate. A song can last for over thirty minutes.

Noisy fishes

Many fishes make sounds by rubbing together their teeth, bones or fin spines. Some even make sounds by moving muscles in their bodies.

This is called a grunt fish. It makes its grunting noise by grinding teeth which grow in its throat.

Scientists think these sounds help the fishes say things to the rest of the group.

Alarm signal

If a minnow is hurt by an attacker, its body sends out a special liquid from the wound.

This signal says "danger" and other minnows keep away.

Dancing fishes

The colorful male guppy fish in this picture is showing the female that he wants to be her mate.

He does this by dancing up to her and fanning out his beautiful fins.

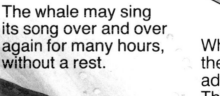

The whale may sing its song over and over again for many hours, without a rest.

Whales change their songs and add new parts. They can even remember a song from one year to the next.

69

Animals and people

For hundreds of years people have trained animals by using a language of signals and commands.

Some kinds of animals are very good at learning what to do and they can be trained to obey human wishes.

Trained to help

Wolves and wild dogs follow their pack leader and do what it tells them. Animals who live or work with people obey a human leader instead.

Dogs can be trained to herd sheep. The farmer whistles signals which tell the dogs what to do.

Some dogs are trained to guide blind people. They obey their owners, but if there is danger the dog gives the orders. If there is something in the way, the dog stops its owner from moving.

Police dog handlers are taught to train their own dogs. The handler and the dog must learn to trust and understand each other.

Sheepdogs are good at their job because their wild relatives herded their prey when they hunted.

This dog is being trained to track down criminals.

70

You and your dog

Dogs are very sensitive. They can tell a lot from small changes in their owner's voice.

When you train a pet dog to obey your words of command, it is the way you say the words which is important.

Monkey helpers

Capuchin monkeys can be trained to help disabled people. One of the jobs they do is brushing hair. The owner tells the helper what to do by speaking or pointing with a special pen.

Visitors must not show their teeth by smiling or grinning. In monkey language this shows anger and the helper may attack.

Koko the gorilla

Most of the time we ask animals to understand our spoken language, but in America a gorilla is being taught a language she can share with humans.

In 1972, Dr. Penny Patterson began teaching American Sign Language to a female gorilla called Koko. They talk with hand signs instead of words.

Koko and Penny are having a tea party. Koko is making the sign for "sip".

Koko tells Penny all kinds of things and even asks her questions. They say how they feel using the same language. When Penny asked Koko "Are you an animal or a person?", Koko answered "Fine animal gorilla".

71

What is my message?

Here are six patterns and shapes. You can find them on animals in this part of the book. Which animals do they belong to? What colors are the patterns and shapes? What are their messages to other animals?

Answers

1. A wasp. This is the yellow and black pattern on its body. The message says "I'm dangerous". 2. A male golden pheasant. This is the yellow and black pattern on its feathery head fan. The message tells a female golden pheasant "look at me". 3. An eyed hawk-moth. These are the black, white and blue eye markings on its wings. They are a trick message saying "I am a big animal". 4. A gull. This is the red spot on its bottom jaw. The message tells the chicks it is feeding time. 5. A peacock. These are the blue, orange, yellow and green markings on its enormous curved feathers. The message tells the peahen "look at me, be my mate". 6. A coral snake. These are the red, black and yellow stripes on its body. The message says "I'm poisonous".

72

WHY DO TIGERS HAVE STRIPES?

Mike Unwin

Designed by Sharon Bennett

Illustrated by Robert Morton, Steven Kirk, Gillian Miller, Robert Gillmor, Treve Tamblin and Stuart Trotter

Editor: Helen Edom

Science consultant: Dr Margaret Rostron

CONTENTS

Additional designs by Non Figg

A world of colors

Many animals, such as tigers, have interesting colors or patterns. This book explains how colors and patterns help all kinds of animals, from the biggest elephants to the tiniest insects.

A tiger has a striped pattern. Can you think of any other animals with stripes?

Matching colors

Different animals' colors often match the places where they live. The oryx is an antelope that lives in the desert. Its pale color matches the sandy background.

In deserts there are few places to hide from enemies. Sandy animals are hard to spot because they blend in. Colors or patterns that help animals to hide are called camouflage.

Some desert animals live in holes. When they come out their sandy-colored camouflage helps them hide from hunters such as hawks and foxes.

An oryx is pale and sandy like the desert.

Scorpion

Gerbil

74

Hidden hunters

Most animals run away if they see a hunter coming. Camouflage helps hunters to hide so they can catch other animals to eat.

Snowy owls live in the Arctic where there is lots of snow. They hunt small creatures called lemmings. The owls' white feathers match the snow. It is hard for lemmings to spot them.

White feathers blend in with the snow and sky.

Lemmings

Forest greens

Many animals that live in rainforests are green to match the colors of the leaves. This camouflage makes them very hard to see.

Look at the green tree frog in this picture. How many other animals can you spot?

Tree frog

Blue waters

Camouflage is also important under the sea. Many sharks and other fish are colored blue or grey. This helps them to blend in with the colors underwater.

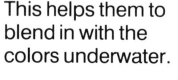

Blue sharks

75

Patterns

Background colors are not the only kind of camouflage. Patterns also help animals to hide.

Breaking up shapes

A tiger in the zoo looks big, bright and easy to see. But in the forests and long grass where it hunts, a tiger can be hard to spot.

A tiger's stripes seem to break up its shape into small pieces. It is hard to see among the patterns and shadows of the background. This helps it to creep up on deer and other animals.

Seeing in black and white

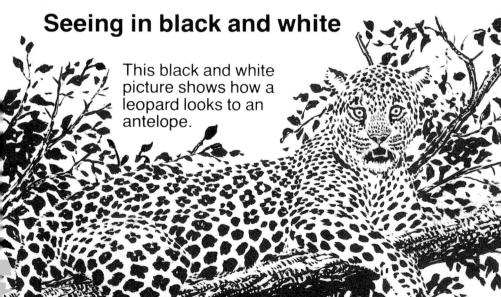

This black and white picture shows how a leopard looks to an antelope.

Many animals such as antelope cannot see colors. They see in black and white. This makes it very hard for them to make out an animal, such as a leopard, whose pattern breaks up its shape.

Lying in wait

The gaboon viper is a snake that lives on the ground in African forests. Its complicated pattern makes its shape hard to see against the leaves.

Small animals cannot see a gaboon viper lying in wait for them. When they get close, the viper kills them with a bite from its poisonous fangs.

From a distance

The ringed plover lives on beaches. Close up its markings look bright. But from a distance you can only see a pattern that looks like the pebbles.

If the plover keeps still, it seems to disappear into the stony background. Enemies cannot spot it unless they are close.

Ringed plover

Seaweed shapes

The sargassum fish has strange lumps of skin that stick out from it body. These make its shape hard to see. It seems to disappear among the seaweed where it lives.

People hiding

Soldiers wear uniforms with special patterns. This helps them to blend into the background, just like tigers do.

77

Shadows and light

Light and shadow can make animals stand out from their background.

Lying flat

This bird is called a stone curlew. It is well camouflaged, but you can still see its shadow. In daylight, solid things always have shadows. This helps you to see where they are.

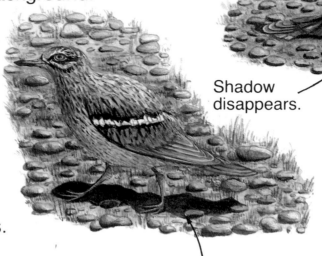

Shadow disappears.

Stone curlew's shadow.

A stone curlew lies flat on the ground so it looks small. This makes its shadow disappear so it is even harder for enemies to spot.

Flat shapes

Some animals have flattened bodies. Enemies do not notice them because they hardly leave any shadow.

Flaps of skin on a gecko's tail make it look flat.

The flying gecko is a lizard that lives on tree trunks. It has a flat body with flaps of skin that press down on the bark. This helps it to hide.

Dark and pale

You can often spot solid things by seeing the light shining on them.

Sunlight makes the top of this rock look lighter than the background.

No sunlight reaches the bottom, so it looks darker than the background.

The impala, like many animals, is colored dark above and pale below. This is the opposite of the natural light and shadow that fall on its body. It makes the impala harder to pick out from its background.

From below

Many water birds such as puffins are white underneath. They swim on the surface of the water and dive down to catch fish.

From underwater the surface looks bright because of sunlight above it. It is hard for fish to spot puffins from below. Their white undersides are hidden against the bright surface of the water.

Hiding with mirrors

Many sea fish such as herrings have shiny silver scales on their sides and bellies. Underwater, these scales work like mirrors. They reflect the colors of the water, so the fish become almost invisible.

79

Disguises

Some animals are shaped to look like other things. This helps them to hide. These insects all have disguises that help them hide in forests.

This caterpillar looks just like a bird dropping, so nothing wants to eat it.

The thorn bug looks just like a thorn on a branch.

The leaf butterfly's folded wings look like a leaf on the forest floor.

The stick insect looks just like twigs.

Standing straight

Animals can help their disguises to work by the way they behave. The tawny frogmouth is a bird with colors like bark. If it is in danger, it points its beak upward so it looks like a dead branch.

Deadly flowers

The flower mantis is a hunting insect. Its body is the same color and shape as the flowers where it hides.

Other insects that visit the flower do not notice the mantis lying in wait to catch them.

Like a log

A crocodile in the water can look just like a floating log. This disguise helps it to catch antelope that come to the water to drink.

The crocodile's rough skin looks like old tree bark.

Dressing up

Some animals disguise themselves by decorating their bodies. The sponge crab lives on the sea bed. It holds a sponge on its back with its back legs.

This helps the crab to look like part of the sea bed.

Antelope do not notice the crocodile drifting towards them. When the crocodile gets close enough, it grabs an antelope with its huge jaws and pulls it into the water.

81

Surprises

Some animals stop enemies attacking by tricking or surprising them. They often use colors or patterns to help.

Frightening eyes

Many hunters are frightened if they suddenly see a big pair of eyes.

This swallowtail caterpillar has patterns that look like eyes. Birds think they belong to a bigger, more dangerous creature, so they leave the caterpillar alone.

The caterpillar's real eyes are hidden under here.

A bright flash

Bark

The red underwing moth looks well camouflaged on bark. But if it is spotted by a bird, it opens its top wings to show the bright red underneath.

A sudden flash of red surprises the bird. It leaves the moth alone.

Missing the target

This hairstreak butterfly has a pattern on its wings that looks like another head. Birds peck at the wings by mistake. This gives the butterfly time to escape.

Head pattern

The real head is at this end.

Puffing up

Some animals make themselves look bigger to trick enemies. A long-eared owl spreads its wings and puffs up its feathers to frighten enemies away.

This owl looks twice as big as usual.

Playing dead

Some hunters, such as hawks, only attack living creatures. An opossum is a small animal that pretends to be dead when it is in danger. When the danger has gone, the opossum gets up again.

An opossum pretends to be dead by rolling over with its mouth open.

Looking both ways

In India tigers sometimes attack farmers. Tigers are scared by people's faces so they attack from behind. Farmers wear masks on the backs of their heads to scare tigers away.

83

Keep-away colors

Some animals do not try to hide. They have bright colors and patterns that are meant to be seen. These colors are a warning to their enemies.

Remembering colors

Black and yellow patterns are easy for animals to remember. Wasps are bright yellow and black. They can give their enemies a painful sting.

Black and yellow are warning colours.

If a young bird is stung by a wasp, it remembers its pattern. It will not try to catch a wasp again, because it knows that black and yellow things hurt.

84

Eating bees

A few birds, such as bee-eaters, have found a way to eat bees safely. They are not put off by warning colors. Bee-eaters bang a bee on a branch so its stinger is squeezed out and broken.

Being seen

Many poisonous animals do not run away. Instead they show off their warning colors to their enemies.

The deadly poisonous arrow-poison frog does not hop away from enemies like other frogs do. It crawls around slowly so it can easily be seen.

Fierce black and white

The ratel is an African badger. Its white back makes it easy to see. Although it is quite small, it is very fierce and is not afraid of any other animal.

The ratel has strong teeth and claws.

Smelly warning

Skunks are small animals with a bold pattern. They can squirt a nasty, smelly liquid at enemies such as dogs.

A spotted skunk stands up on its front legs to show its pattern. This warns the dog to stay back. If the dog comes closer, the skunk sprays it.

The ratel does not need to keep a look-out for danger like most animals do. Its colors warn enemies that it is too dangerous to attack.

Signals for people

People use colors just like animals do. Red often means "hot", "stop" or "danger".

This red tap warns you to be careful because the water is hot.

85

Copying colors

Some animals survive because they have colors and patterns that help them to look like other kinds of animals.

Coral snake

Poisonous or safe?

Can you tell the difference between these two snakes? The coral snake is very poisonous. Its bright colors are a warning.

The king snake looks like a coral snake, but it is not poisonous at all. If you look hard you can see that its pattern is slightly different.

King snake

Other animals are afraid to attack the king snake because it looks like a poisonous coral snake.

Which is the wasp?

Some insects look just like wasps even though they do not really have stings. Most animals do not attack these insects because their colors remind them of stinging wasps.

Can you guess which insect is a wasp? Look on page 148 for the answer.

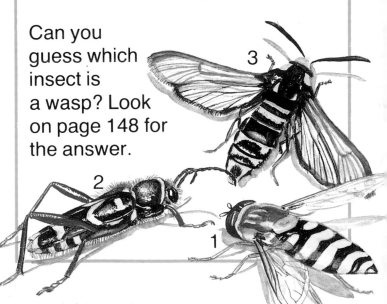

Ant antics

Most animals leave ants alone because they bite and sting. Some kinds of spider look and behave like ants to fool their enemies.

Ants

The spider holds up two of its eight legs so it appears to have only six legs, like an ant.

The spider's upright front legs look like an ant's feelers.

Getting close

The cleaner fish helps bigger fish by cleaning unwanted dirt and lice from their skin.

Cleaner fish

The sabre-toothed blenny looks like a cleaner fish, but it is really a hunter that tricks other fish.

Sabre-toothed blenny

Big fish let the blenny come near because they think it is a cleaner fish. But the blenny attacks them and takes bites out of their fins.

Whose egg?

Can you tell which of these eggs is the odd one out?

Reed warbler

The middle one is a cuckoo's egg. The rest belong to the reed warbler.

The cuckoo lays its egg in a reed warbler's nest. It is the same color as the eggs that are already there. The warblers think the cuckoo's egg is their own so they look after it.

Signals

Some kinds of animals use colors and patterns as signals to each other.

Danger

A rabbit has a short, fluffy, white tail. If it sees an enemy such as a fox, it runs quickly back to its burrow, flashing its tail in the air.

The white tail is a signal to other rabbits. It says "danger!"

Follow my leader

Ring-tailed lemurs are animals with long black and white tails. When a group of lemurs is on the move, they hold their tails up like flags.

Lemurs' tails help them to see each other and stay together. They are signals that say "follow me".

Getting angry

A tiger has bold, white spots on its ears. If one tiger is angry with another, it turns the backs of its ears forwards to show the white spots.

The white spots are a signal that warns other tigers to keep away.

Looking different

Colors can make it easier to tell similar animals apart. This helps animals to recognize others of their own kind.

These are the wings of two different finches. Their shape and size are the same, but the patterns and colors help to tell them apart.

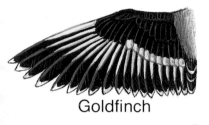

Goldfinch

Chaffinch

Being fed

Baby birds in nests wait for their parents to bring food. The babies' mouths are brightly colored inside.

These baby great tits have bright orange mouths.

When a parent arrives with food, the babies open their mouths wide to show the color inside. This is a signal to the parent. It says "feed me!"

People's colors

People also use colors to tell each other apart. All sports teams wear their own colors. This stops them getting mixed up with each other.

Different colored shirts help two soccer teams to tell each other apart.

Mysterious lights

Hatchet fish live deep at the bottom of the sea, where it is very dark. They have small patches on their bodies that light up and flash on and off.

Scientists think these lights could be signals to help hatchet fish recognize each other.

Showing off

Many male animals have bright colors to make them look attractive to females. This helps to bring the male and female together to breed.

Bright or brown

Male and female birds often look different from each other.

A male golden pheasant has beautifully colored feathers which he shows off to attract a female.

The female pheasant has more dull colors. This helps her to hide when she is protecting her eggs and chicks.

Risky colors

Bright colors can also attract enemies. In spring a male paradise whydah's bright colors are easy to spot, and his long tail makes it hard for him to fly away.

After the whydah has found a female he loses his colors and long tail. For the rest of the year he stays plain brown.

Putting on a show

Some male birds put on a show to attract females. Every spring, male ruffs gather together. They puff up their feathers and fight. Females choose the males that put on the best show.

Three different male ruffs fighting.

Colorful lizards

A male anolis lizard has an orange flap of skin under this throat. Usually it is folded up. But sometimes the lizard puffs it out and nods his head to show off the color.

The bright throat attracts females. It also warns other males to keep out of the area.

Fierce faces

Mandrills are African monkeys. A male mandrill has a colorful face that gets brighter when he is looking for a female. The biggest and fiercest males are brightest of all.

A female mandrill chooses the male with the brightest colors. Other males keep away from him.

Collecting color

A male bowerbird attracts a female by building a pile of twigs called a bower. He then decorates it with shells, flowers and bright, shiny things.

A female bowerbird chooses the male with the best bower. The pair then build a nest together.

91

Making colors

Fur, feathers, scales and skin can be all sorts of different colors. Animals get these colors in many different ways.

Colors from food

Flamingos' feathers are pink because of a coloring called carotene which is found in water plants. Flamingos get carotene by eating tiny water animals that feed on these plants.

Often flamingos in zoos are not as pink as wild ones, because there is not enough carotene in their food.

Shiny colors

Many birds, such as sunbirds, have bright, shiny feathers. These change color when light falls on them from different directions.

This sunbird's feathers change from blue to green as the light shines on them.

Killed for colors

Some snakes are becoming rare because people kill them for their beautiful skins.

This bag is made from the skin of a python.

Growing green

Animals do not normally grow green fur. But this sloth looks green. This is because tiny green plants called algae grow in its fur.

Jigsaw

Butterflies' patterns are made by thousands of tiny different-colored scales that fit together.

Peacock butterfly scales

This is how the wing of a peacock butterfly looks close up. Can you see how the scales are arranged in rows?

Black fur

Animals have a kind of coloring in their bodies called melanin. Melanin makes dark colors in fur and skin.

A black panther is really a leopard born with more melanin than usual. Its fur is black. But if you look closely you can still see its spots.

White all over

Sometimes animals are born white. They have no melanin so they cannot make dark colors. These are called albino animals.

An albino blackbird has white feathers.

93

Changes

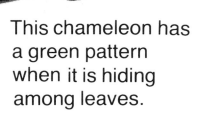

Some animals can change their colors. Chameleons are lizards that change the color of their skin to match different backgrounds.

This chameleon has a green pattern when it is hiding among leaves.

On sandy ground the same chameleon turns brown. It is always very hard to spot.

Sole survivor

The sole is a flatfish. It hides from enemies by lying flat on the sea bed. Its color depends on where it lies.

This sole is the color and pattern of the pebbles on which it is lying. If it moves onto the sand, it becomes sandy-colored.

Sudden changes

If an octopus is in danger, different colors flash over its body. This surprises enemies and gives the octopus time to escape.

Colors also show how an octopus feels. For example, an angry octopus often turns red.

White for winter

Many animals that live in cold parts of the world turn white in winter. At the end of summer an Arctic fox sheds its brown fur and grows a white coat.

Fox in summer   Fox in winter

White fur helps the fox to hide during winter when the ground is covered in snow. In spring the fox's brown fur grows back again.

After the fire

In Africa, fires often change the color of grassland by burning it black. Some kinds of grasshopper can turn from green to black to match the color of the ground.

Before the fire the grasshoppers were green like this one.

Colors of the land

The color of an African elephant's skin can change, depending on the soil where it lives. This is because it covers itself in dirt and mud to cool down.

This elephant lives in a place with red soil, so it has reddish skin.

Animal puzzle

Here are eight different parts and patterns from animals that you can find in this part of the book.

Can you figure out which animals they come from? The answers are at the bottom of the page.

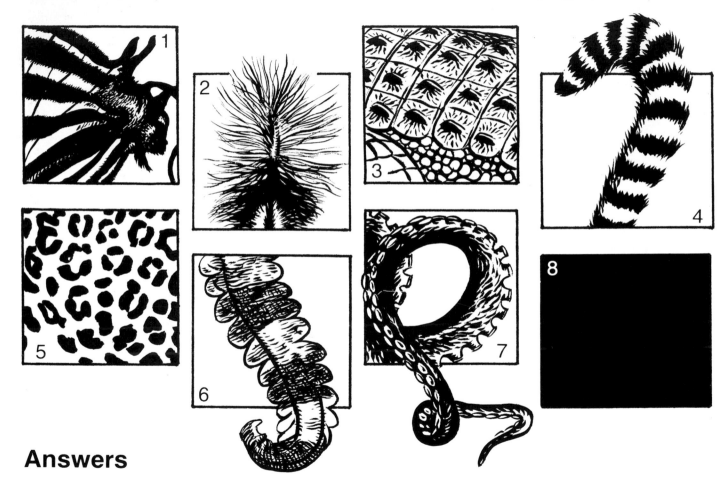

Answers

1. Hairstreak butterfly 2. Spotted skunk 3. Crocodile 4. Ring-tailed lemur 5. Leopard 6. Flying gecko 7. Octopus 8. Black panther on a dark night.

WHAT MAKES A FLOWER GROW?

Susan Mayes

Designed by Mike Pringle
Illustrated by Brin Edwards and Mike Pringle
Series editor: Heather Amery

CONTENTS

All about flowers

Thousands of different flowers grow all over the world. They grow in gardens, on vegetables, on trees, in streets, in hedges and in your home.

Flowers are all kinds of colors, shapes and sizes. Some of them have very strong smells.

Insects and other tiny animals visit them. Most flowers die each year and grow again later.

Some flowers live in very hot countries and others live in cold places. Very strange flowers grow in some parts of the world.

Why do flowers have different colors and smells? Why do they grow again and what do they need to grow well?

What are the strangest flowers? You can find out about all of these things in this part of the book.

Taking a close look

If you look closely at a flower, you can see that it has different parts. Each part has a special job.

Looking at a poppy

A baby flower, called a bud, grows safely inside two sepals.

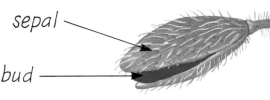

sepal

bud

Sepals protect the bud and stop birds and insects from eating it.

petal

As the bud grows, it opens up and the petals stretch out.

The stigma is sticky. It grows on top of the pistil.

The pistil is in the middle of the flower. New seeds will grow inside. It is sometimes called the seed box.

pistil

stigma

stamen

The stamens grow around the pistil.

On top of each stamen there are tiny specks of golden dust, called pollen.

Different flowers

Most flowers have the same main parts, but they are all kinds of different colors, shapes and sizes.

A yellow water lily has big sepals around the outside and lots of short petals in the middle.

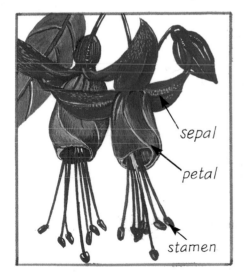

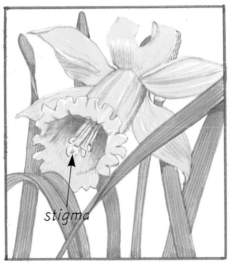

Fuchsias have long stamens and colorful sepals and petals.

A daffodil has one long stigma which grows from the pistil.

The petals of the snapdragon are all joined together.

Who visits a flower?

Flowers all over the world are visited by small animals, birds and many kinds of insects.

Most animals go to flowers to look for pollen and sweet liquid food inside, called nectar.

Tiny birds

A hummingbird hovers in front of brightly colored flowers to drink he nectar with its long beak.

Bats

In some countries, bats fly to flowers which open in the evening. They search for nectar and pollen.

Honey bees visit all kinds of flowers, looking for food to store for the winter.

Butterflies settle on buddleia flowers to drink nectar with their long tongues.

A bumble bee crawls into a foxglove to find the sweet food.

Flower signals

Many flowers use special signals which make the insects and tiny creatures come to visit them.

Colors

Special colors and markings guide bees to flowers and show them where to find the pollen inside.

You cannot see some markings but bees can. They do not see colors and shapes the same way as we do.

Smells

Most flowers have a sweet smell. It comes from the petals and tells visitors there is food nearby.

Honeysuckle has a strong smell at night. This is when the moths come out to find nectar for food.

A nasty smell

Flies visit a stapelia flower to lay their eggs. They come because it looks and smells like rotting meat.

Visitors at work

Insects and other small animals help plants when visiting them for food.

They carry pollen from flower to flower. This will make seeds grow.

When a bee lands on a flower, some pollen from the stamens rubs off on to its body.

The bee flies to the next flower and some pollen rubs off on to the flower's stigma.

More pollen sticks to the bee as it crawls around on each flower it visits.

Open or closed

Flowers are not open to visitors if the weather is bad. They close to keep the pollen dry and safe.

A day-time flower closes up its petals at night to stop the dew from wetting the pollen inside.

Pollen in the air

Some plants do not need visitors. They do not have special colors or smells because their pollen is carried from plant to plant by the wind.

Tiny grains

Some trees have flowers called catkins. Their tiny, golden grains of pollen blow away in the wind.

Grass has flowers at the top of the stalk. The pollen is high up so it blows away easily.

Pollen clouds

In the summer, you sometimes see clouds of pollen in the air. People with hay fever sneeze and sneeze.

Did you know?

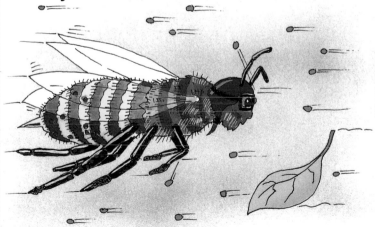

Pollen grains carried by flower visitors are sticky, but pollen grains in the air are smooth and dry.

All about seeds

A plant cannot grow seeds until pollen reaches its stigma. And the pollen must be from the same kind of plant.

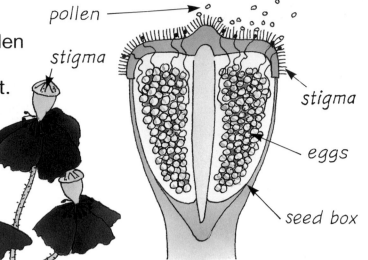

pollen

stigma

stigma

eggs

seed box

Grains of pollen, carried by visitors, or blown by the wind, land on a new flower. They stick to the stigma.

The grains travel down into the tiny eggs inside the seed box. They make the eggs grow into seeds.

stamen

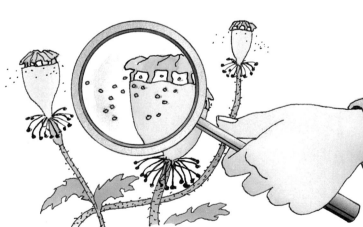

The flower does not need the petals and stamens any more, so they drop off. Only the seed box is left.

The seeds grow inside until they are ripe. The seeds of this plant leave through small holes.

106

Kinds of seeds

Many different plants have seeds which you can eat.

Sweet chestnuts, walnuts and coconuts are three kinds of seeds which come from trees.

Sunflower seeds are used to make oil and margarine. You can also eat them from the flower.

Inside and outside

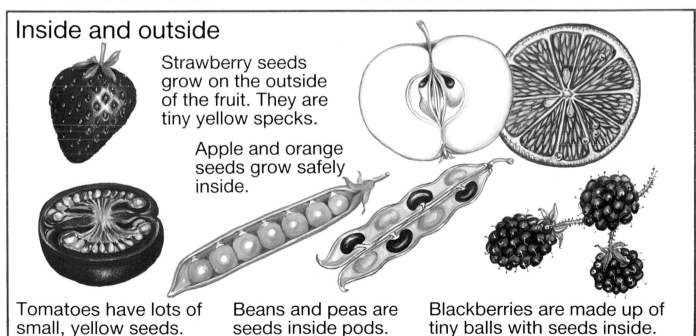

Strawberry seeds grow on the outside of the fruit. They are tiny yellow specks.

Apple and orange seeds grow safely inside.

Tomatoes have lots of small, yellow seeds.

Beans and peas are seeds inside pods.

Blackberries are made up of tiny balls with seeds inside.

Seeds on the move

Popping out

The seeds of an iris grow inside colorful, round fruit. When the fruit is ripe, the seeds leave by popping out on to the ground.

Old Man's Beard

This is the name for the big, fluffy balls from a clematis plant. They are carried by the wind, with the seeds inside.

Seeds leave plants in different ways. Most of them are blown in the wind or are carried by animals.

Birds like to eat brightly colored seeds. They carry them away.

Seeds with hooks or sticky hairs, stick to birds and animals.

Conkers are the seeds of horse chestnut trees. They fall to the ground in green, spiky cases.

Seeds from a sycamore tree spin to the ground like helicopters.

Dandelion seeds blow away in the wind.

When poppy seeds are ripe, they pop out of the pod.

Ants carry some seeds away and store them for winter food.

Many of the seeds will die or be eaten but some are covered by soil or leaves. They stay there all winter until spring comes.

Rolling along

Tumbleweeds grow in America. When their seeds are ripe the plant curls into a ball. It rolls along in the wind, scattering the seeds.

The fastest seeds

A plant called the Squirting Cucumber squirts its seeds out. They travel at about 100km (60 miles) an hour.

Roots and shoots

In the spring, days grow longer and warmer. Seeds get the warmth and rain they need to make them grow.

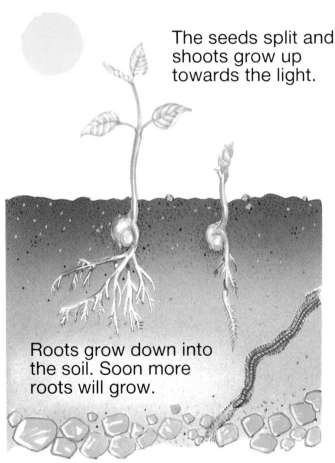

The seeds split and shoots grow up towards the light.

Roots grow down into the soil. Soon more roots will grow.

The roots feed the plant with water and goodness from the soil. They also hold the plant in the ground.

Leaves and sunlight

Little seed leaves feed the plant until the big leaves grow. Leaves have a special way of using air and sunlight to make plant food.

Growing beans

Put some paper towels in a jar with some water.

Put some beans next to the glass.

Put the jar in a warm, light place. The beans will swell up until they split and sprout roots and shoots.

Waterways

Plants suck up the water they need through their waterways. These are very thin tubes inside the stems.

Try this

You will need:

a big jar
some food dye
some white flowers

In the soil

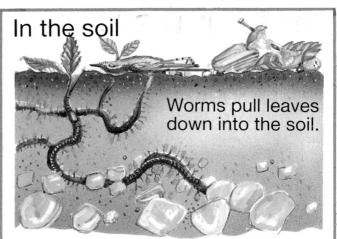

Worms pull leaves down into the soil.

Soil is full of things which are good for plants. Dead leaves, plants and tiny creatures rot away and make good plant food.

Put some water in the jar and add a few drops of food dye. Stand the flowers in it. After a few days the petal tips will change color.

In two more days, the flowers will be the same color as the dye. This is because the flowers suck the water and dye up into the petals.

Things you can grow

You can buy packets of flower and vegetable seeds in the shops. Here are some of the things you will need when you plant seeds for yourself.

plant pots or yogurt cups
a bag of compost
a small watering can or jug
a little trowel or an old spoon
a plate and some kitchen towels
cress and sunflower seeds

Compost is a special soil with rich plant food in it.

Growing cress

Cress grows very easily and quickly at any time of the year.

Your cress will be ready to eat when it is about 7cm (2½in) high.

You do not need soil, just some damp kitchen towels on a plate. Sprinkle some cress seeds on top.

Put the plate in a light place. The tiny shoots will soon grow, but you must keep the towels damp.

Sunflowers

In the spring you can start to grow sunflower seeds in pots.

Use a pot of compost for each seed. Push the seed in and sprinkle a little compost on top. Water the pots and put them in a warm, sunny place.

Try measuring the sunflowers to see how tall they grow.

After a few weeks shoots will appear and the plants will grow bigger. When they have four leaves they are big enough to plant in the garden.

Remember

Plants need these things to help them grow well.

They need sunlight to help them make their own special plant food.

They need water, but not too much, or they may rot.

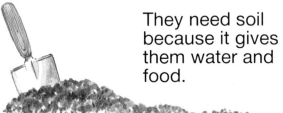

They need soil because it gives them water and food.

Where flowers grow

In the town

Gardens and parks are not the only places in towns where you might find flowers growing.

Some seeds are blown on to the roofs, where they grow.

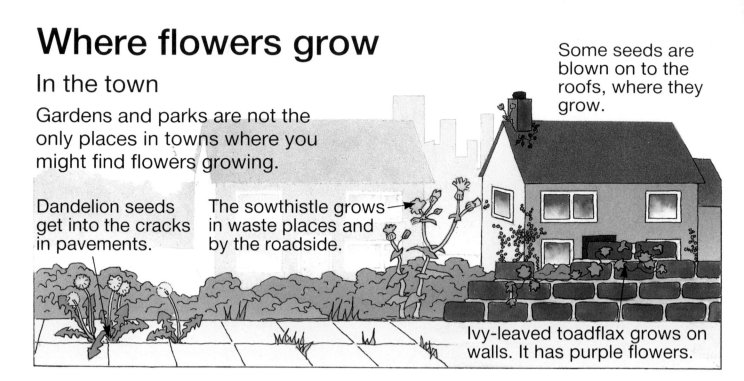

Dandelion seeds get into the cracks in pavements.

The sowthistle grows in waste places and by the roadside.

Ivy-leaved toadflax grows on walls. It has purple flowers.

In the country

Many wild flowers grow in different countries all over the world. These flowers grow in Europe.

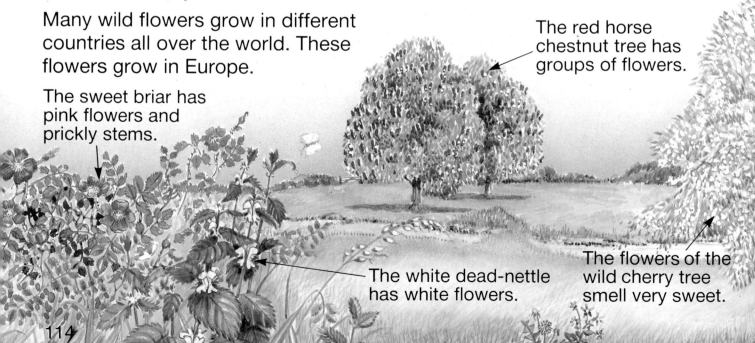

The red horse chestnut tree has groups of flowers.

The sweet briar has pink flowers and prickly stems.

The white dead-nettle has white flowers.

The flowers of the wild cherry tree smell very sweet.

In hot places

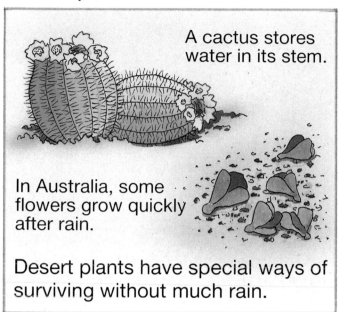

A cactus stores water in its stem.

In Australia, some flowers grow quickly after rain.

Desert plants have special ways of surviving without much rain.

In cold places

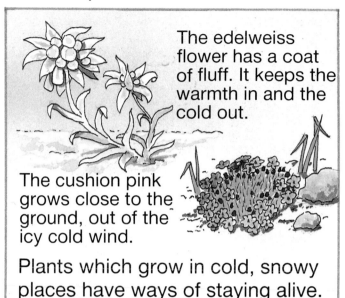

The edelweiss flower has a coat of fluff. It keeps the warmth in and the cold out.

The cushion pink grows close to the ground, out of the icy cold wind.

Plants which grow in cold, snowy places have ways of staying alive.

By the water

Some flowers grow well by the sea, by streams and other damp places.

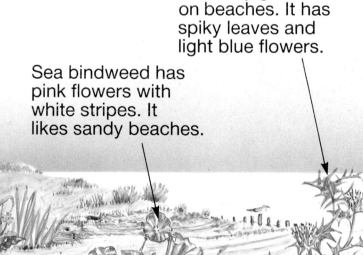

Sea holly grows on beaches. It has spiky leaves and light blue flowers.

The marsh marigold likes ditches and wet places.

Sea bindweed has pink flowers with white stripes. It likes sandy beaches.

Water crowfoot → floats on top of the water.

115

Amazing plant facts

Many strange plants and flowers grow in parts of the world. They are all sorts of amazing shapes and sizes. Some even eat small animals.

The biggest flowers

The rafflesia flower is also very smelly.

The flower of the rafflesia plant is the biggest in the world. It is nearly a metre (3 feet) across.

The giant cactus

The saguaro is the largest cactus in the world. It grows as high as 15 meters (49 feet).

Tiny plants

The smallest flowering plant is a kind of duckweed. It is so tiny that it looks like scum on the water.

Flower traps

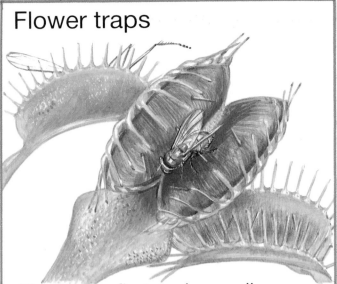

The venus fly trap has spiky leaves. They snap shut to catch insects and tiny animals inside.

The sundew plant has leaves with sticky blobs. Insects stick to them and are eaten as plant food.

The oldest potted plant

A man grew a plant in a pot in Vienna in 1801. It is still alive and will soon be 200 years old.

The strongest water lily

The victoria amazonica water lily is strong enough for a child to stand on its thick, floating leaves.

Useful words

Here are some plant words. The pictures will help you remember what they are.

hay fever

People with hay fever sneeze when there is a lot of pollen in the air.

insect

This is a small animal with 6 legs and a body made of 3 parts. A bee is an insect.

nectar

This is sweet liquid food inside a flower. Small visitors come to drink it. Bees use it to make honey.

pistil

New seeds grow in this part of the flower. It is also called the seed box.

pollen

This is the name for tiny golden specks on a flower. It makes new seeds grow in another flower.

roots

These parts of a plant grow down into the ground. They take in water and goodness from the soil.

sepals

These wrap around a bud to keep it safe while it is growing.

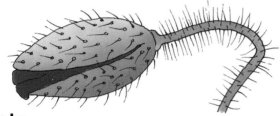

shoots

These are the new parts of a plant.

stamen

This part of a flower has pollen at the end.

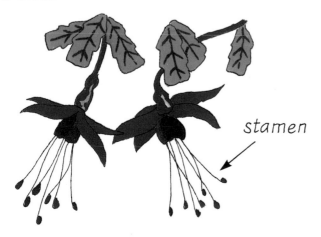

stamen

stem

This is the stalk of a plant. It holds the flowers up, above the ground.

stigma

This flower part is sticky. Pollen from another flower sticks to it easily.

stigma

waterways

These are thin tubes inside a plant stem. The plant drinks water through them, to stay alive and to grow.

119

Flower puzzle

Here are 10 different kinds of flowers. They are all in this part of the book.

Can you find them and learn their names? The answers are at the bottom of this page.

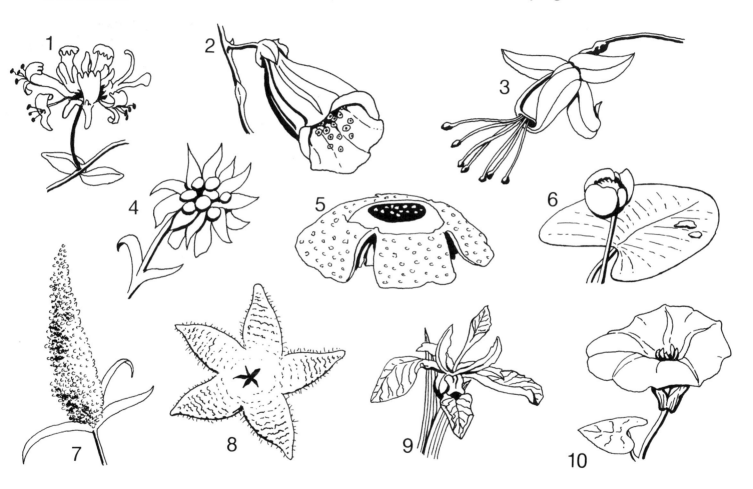

Answers

1. honeysuckle 2. foxglove 3. fuchsia 4. edelweiss 5. rafflesia 6. yellow water lily 7. buddleia 8. stapelia 9. iris 10. sea bindweed

120

HOW DO BEES MAKE HONEY?

Anna Claybourne

Designed by Lindy Dark

Illustrated by Sophie Allington and Annabel Spenceley

Edited by Kamini Khanduri

Scientific consultant: James Hamill
(The Hive Honey Shop, London)

CONTENTS

Additional illustrations by Janos Marffy

Bees and other insects

Bees are amazing insects. There are lots of different kinds, but honeybees are the most common - and they are the ones that make honey. Here, you can find out about honeybees, and about other insects.

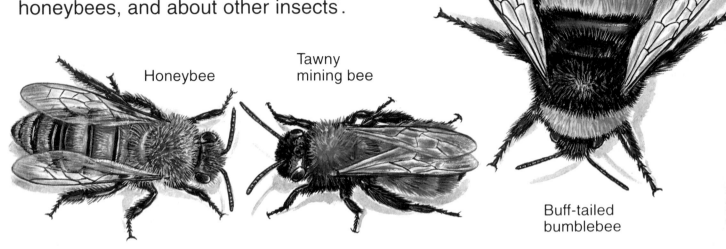

Honeybee

Tawny mining bee

Buff-tailed bumblebee

Busy bees

Some people are frightened of honeybees, because they can sting. In fact, bees are usually busy looking for flowers, and don't sting very often.

Bees only sting if they are frightened. If you leave them alone, they probably won't hurt you.

Bees make delicious honey. On page 127, you can find out how.

Insects all around

There are over a million kinds of insects. They live in all sorts of places - in the ground, on plants, under stones, and even in houses.

Honeybees fly from flower to flower, collecting food.

You can often see houseflies inside houses.

Butterflies fly around plants.

There are many different kinds of beetles. Some live on trees.

Dragonflies live near watery places.

These ants dig tunnels in the ground to live in.

123

A closer look

This picture shows a honeybee ten times bigger than in real life. You can see the different parts of its body.

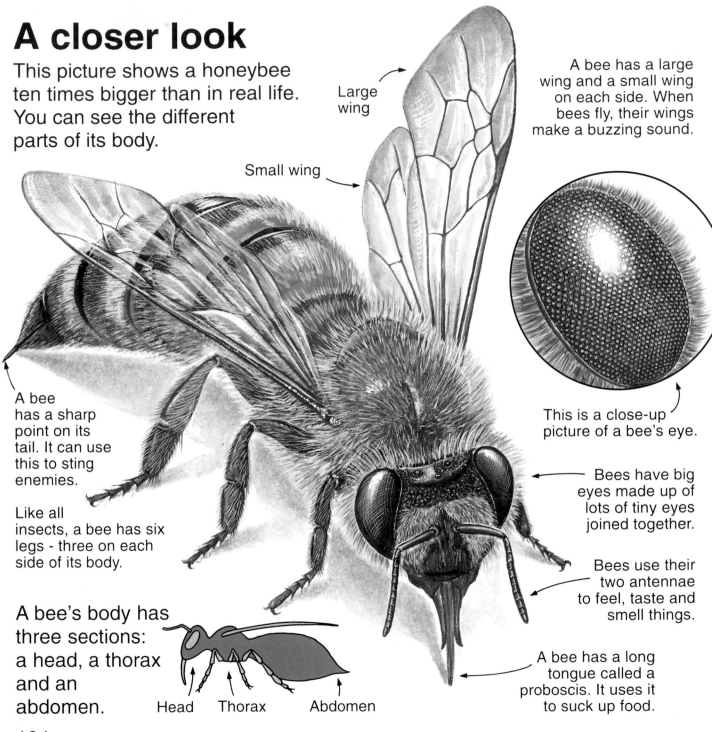

Large wing

Small wing

A bee has a large wing and a small wing on each side. When bees fly, their wings make a buzzing sound.

This is a close-up picture of a bee's eye.

A bee has a sharp point on its tail. It can use this to sting enemies.

Like all insects, a bee has six legs - three on each side of its body.

Bees have big eyes made up of lots of tiny eyes joined together.

Bees use their two antennae to feel, taste and smell things.

A bee's body has three sections: a head, a thorax and an abdomen.

Head   Thorax   Abdomen

A bee has a long tongue called a proboscis. It uses it to suck up food.

A bee or not a bee?

Lots of insects have black and yellow stripes. People sometimes mix them up with bees. Only one of these is a honeybee. Can you tell which one?

① ③ ⑤ ② ④

Look on page 148 for the answer.

Bees at home

Honeybees live together in big groups called colonies. Today, most colonies live in beehives built by people.

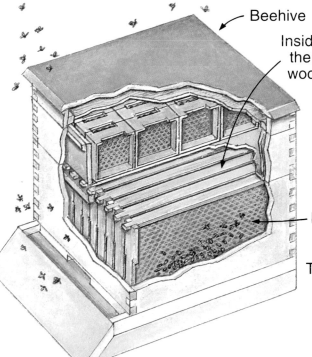

Beehive

Inside a beehive, there are lots of wooden frames.

The bees build a wax honeycomb in each frame. They store their honey there.

There can be over 50,000 bees living in one hive.

Wild bees' nests often hang from branches.

Some honeybees live in the wild. They build honeycomb nests out of wax.

125

Honey

The honey you buy in shops all comes from honeybees. They make honey as food for themselves and their babies. People take some of the honey, but they leave enough for the bees.

Honey milk shake

To make this milk shake, measure out a cupful of milk. Add a scoop of ice-cream and two teaspoons of honey.

Whisk or blend the mixture. Pour it into a glass.

Top with banana slices.

Collecting honey

People who keep bees and collect their honey are called beekeepers. They wear gloves and veils when they are working, so they do not get stung. Their clothes are white, because this makes the bees feel calm.

The beekeeper lifts each frame out of the hive, takes out the honey and puts the frame back.

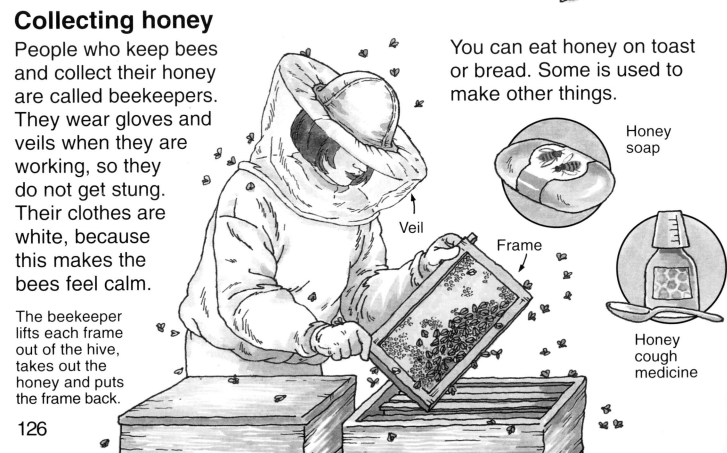

Veil

Frame

You can eat honey on toast or bread. Some is used to make other things.

Honey soap

Honey cough medicine

How bees make honey

Honeybees make honey from a sweet liquid called nectar, which they suck out of flowers. Older bees collect the nectar and pass it on to younger bees.

Passing on nectar

This picture shows how bees make honey inside their bodies.

Honey sac

The nectar goes down a tube to the bee's stomach, or honey sac.

In the honey sac, the nectar gets thicker and turns into honey.

The honey comes out through the bee's mouth. It is kept safe in the hive.

Different kinds

Different kinds of honey come from different flowers.

Apple blossom honey is thick and yellow.

Borage flower honey is pale and runny.

Next time you go to the shops, you could look for different kinds of honey. How many can you find?

Bees and flowers

On warm days, female honeybees visit flowers to collect nectar and a kind of yellow powder called pollen. They use pollen as food for their babies.

The bee lands on the flower and sticks her proboscis, or tongue, into the middle to reach the nectar.

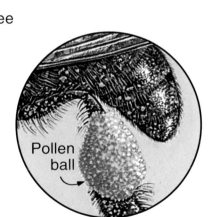

Honeybee

Pollen ball

Petals

Tiny drops of nectar are hidden in little hollows at the bottom of the flower's petals.

Pollen is found on little stalks, called stamens, in the middle of the flower.

Some pollen sticks to the bee's legs and body. She rolls it into balls which she carries on her back legs.

128

Busy helpers

Flowers need to swap pollen with each other to grow seeds. Bees and other insects carry pollen from one flower to the next. This is called pollination.

This bumblebee is visiting a dog rose. Her fur gets covered in specks of pollen.

When the bumblebee flies to another dog rose, she carries some pollen with her.

The pollen helps the second dog rose make seeds which can grow into new dog roses.

Making a beeline

Many flowers have bright markings and strong smells. These attract insects to pollinate the flowers. Some flowers also have dark lines called honeyguides.

Mountain pansy →

Honeyguides →

Scientists think that honeyguides may help insects find their way into flowers.

Flower feeders

It's not just bees that like flowers. Many other insects, such as butterflies, visit flowers to feed on nectar.

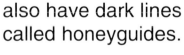

Monarch butterfly feeding on nectar

Inside a beehive

This picture shows part of a honeycomb inside a beehive. It is made up of lots of little compartments called cells. There are three types of honeybees in a hive.

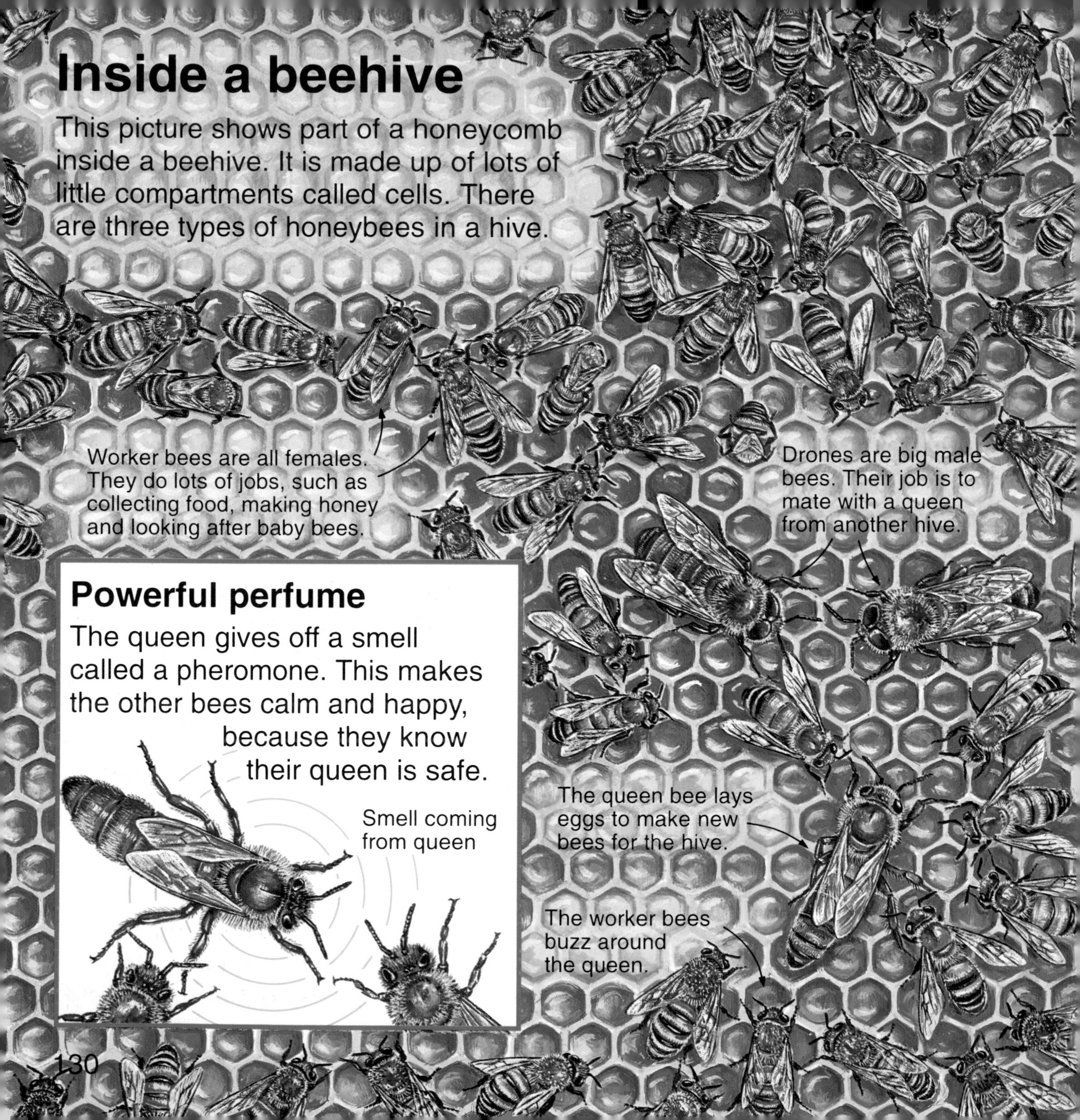

Worker bees are all females. They do lots of jobs, such as collecting food, making honey and looking after baby bees.

Drones are big male bees. Their job is to mate with a queen from another hive.

Powerful perfume

The queen gives off a smell called a pheromone. This makes the other bees calm and happy, because they know their queen is safe.

Smell coming from queen

The queen bee lays eggs to make new bees for the hive.

The worker bees buzz around the queen.